GRAND COVEN

Grand Coven

AN INLAND SEA
NOVEL

Shanon L. Mayer

Shanon Mayer

For everyone who helped support and
encourage me along this journey.
Thanks for reminding me that there is
still magic to be found in the world.
Special thanks to Joe and Patti for
getting me through the tough parts.
This story would not have been the same
without both of you.

Books by Shanon L. Mayer

Chronicles of the Chosen
Sphere of Power
Veil of Deception
Reflections of Doubt
Palace of Stone

Jen Rice novels
Captives and Prisoners
Festival of Souls
Beautiful Monsters

Inland Sea
Star of Darkness
Eyes of Midnight
Grand Coven

Shadow Tribunal
Diamond Queen

1

"Remember, students, care is key." Magi Tanis, the mental arts instructor, paced across the front of the classroom. "Do not rush, take as long as you need because this kind of magic can never be rushed."

Not for the first time, Ahna wondered if she was in the wrong field. Memory enhancement and retrieval no longer seemed as exciting as it had when she had been a first-year student and it was a lot more difficult than she had anticipated. Where she had envisioned with excitement being able to read minds and knowing what people were going to do before *they* even knew what they were going to do, there was a lot more drudgery than just that. Despite how useful the mental arts would be in her future, she simply wasn't excited for it anymore. Perhaps she should change her field to illusions or perhaps enchantment. She wasn't particularly good at enchantments but illusions had come relatively easy to her.

Ahna was only a few days shy of her eighteenth birthday, the third she would be spending away from her family. The first had been hard, the second much easier and this year, she planned to do her best to not even consider it. Instead, she intended to focus on her training so that she could get good marks on the year-end testing. Birthdays were for children, after all. Once one reached the age of adulthood, there was little to be had by experiencing more of them.

As with all of the students at the Three Rivers Academy of Magic, she wore black training robes. First year students had a red sash at the collar, second years had orange. As a third year, Ahna had yellow. The sash complemented her golden hair, which hung over her shoulders in soft waves, held out of her face by a pair of golden hair combs inlaid with pearls, a good-luck gift from her mother when she had left for the Academy. As with everyone in her family, her eyes were sea green, an uncommon trait back home and even more rare in the Inland Sea area where the Academy was located.

Not that choosing a field for specialization mattered, she knew. Once she finished her studies and returned home, her father was certain to marry her off to cement some alliance or another. She would likely be called upon to perform small magical feats to impress her future family or the other members of nobility at the thousands of gatherings she would be forced to attend, both in service to her father and then to her new husband. Should she manage to master the mental arts, then her required presence at the hundreds of social events to which her family was inevitably invited would be put to use as she would become the family spy, a pretty and unassuming mage who could tell who was lying and who was telling the truth. Unappealing as that was, she understood it to be her best-case scenario. Worst-case scenario was that she wouldn't be allowed to use her magic at all after she was married.

"What do we do if the subject isn't willing?" Kerry, one of his students, asked. Kerry was a second-year student, as evidenced by her orange collar sash, and was likely still trying to determine her field. She had short hair the color of stale chocolate, bright blue eyes, and a perpetual scowl. Unlike most of the other students, Kerry always wore polish on her fingernails, today was a deep crimson red.

In the three years Ahna had been a student at the Academy, this was the first class she had been in with Kerry, which was surprising given the small numbers of students in the mental magic field. Although they had only been in class together for a few weeks, Ahna was not impressed with her. The girl was argumentative and hostile to everyone, both students and teachers.

Magi Tanis turned his gaze toward the questioner and then over the rest of the class. "You should all know the answer to that by now," he answered. "Mind magic should never be used on the unwilling." The mental arts instructor was a portly man with a halo of white hair surrounding a bald head. His eyes were deep brown and while they normally sparkled with humor, on that particular day he just looked tired. Dark circles shone beneath his eyes and even his customary bow tie was slightly wilted.

"But what if the subject is a spy or something,

someone you need to interrogate," Kerry persisted. "I'm sure there are times where consent isn't an option."

Slowly nodding, Magi Tanis turned his attention fully to the questioning student. "There are indeed exceptions to this rule but those exceptions are few and far between." His eyes narrowed as he continued. "Not that you will ever have to worry about that, as the power level required to bypass the defenses of an unwilling subject requires far more magical power than you currently possess."

Kerry glared at the instructor and then around at the other students, searching for the source of the snickering.

Ahna shook her thoughts back to the task at hand. Poking around inside the mind of another person was hard enough to begin with; if she didn't focus, she could do real damage.

One of the first things that students at the Academy were taught was to stay within the bounds of their own magical power. If overused, or used too quickly, the mage's body would pay the price. Ahna had seen firsthand an overly eager first-year student drop into a coma for almost a week after over-extending his magical resources. Even after waking back up again, the young student had required almost two months before his magic was restored enough to perform even the most basic of spells.

"What about power boost talismans?" another student asked. This time it was a young man named Phalant. "I understand those can be used to increase the mage's power beyond what they would normally be capable of."

Ahna wasn't sure what Phalant was doing in the same class as she. One of the brightest students Ahna had yet met in the school, she had thought he was specializing in enchantment. At least, that was how it had seemed in the handful of enchantment classes she had taken with him. Unlike herself, enchanting items had appeared to come easy to the quiet boy. His collar sash indicated that he was a year ahead of Ahna, the green color contrasted nicely with his dark complexion.

"For many things, yes, a power boosting talisman can help to increase your power," Magi Tanis agreed as he walked to the other side of the room to lean against his podium, "but there is also the question of damage to the subject. By pressing too hard, you can permanently damage the subject, even destroying completely the memories you are trying to access."

Ahna was relieved when class was over. She had been running late that morning and skipped breakfast to make up time. As a result, she was far hungrier than she normally would have been as lunch time finally arrived.

Three Rivers Academy was a massive complex, with two towers stretching high into the clouds with sun-bleached brick walkways suspended between the buildings every hundred feet or so. The walkways were wide enough for five people to stand abroad comfortably and ended in wide balconies where they attached to the buildings. Somehow, trees grew on the balconies despite not having enough room below for the roots to hold. Ahna suspected that nature mages were responsible for that feat. She took her lunch to one of the balconies where a bench sat among a pair of trees, one of her favorite places to eat and view the town almost four hundred feet below. A light wind was blowing, sending the leaves of the trees trembling and dislodging a few to drift to the ground below. She turned into the wind, enjoying the gentle caress across her face.

"Thought I might find you here," a young woman wearing training robes and a purple collar sat down on the bench next to Ahna. During Ahna's first year at the Academy, a third-year student named Zavala had been assigned to her as a student mentor to show her around the campus and keep her from getting lost, as well as to answer any questions Ahna had. They had hit it off immediately and became virtually inseparable. Now, three years later, Ahna and Zavala were the closest of friends.

Zavala was tall, well over Ahna's five feet and four, with warm brown eyes, a smattering of freckles across her nose and cheeks, and a crest of shockingly blue hair that was more feather than hair due to a failed transmutation ritual a few months before. Thankfully, her natural brown hair was beginning to show among the feathers but Ahna knew that there was still much time before the spell wore off completely and her friend returned to normal.

"Hey, Zavvie," she greeted the new arrival. "What's on your mind?" Although she normally preferred to eat her meals in peace and quiet, one of the main reasons she had found the bench outside to begin with, Zavala was one of the few people whose presence didn't bother her.

"Final testing is a nightmare," Zavala groaned. As a sixth-year student, this was Zavala's final year at the Academy. In order to find a good employer after graduation, all of the sixth-year students were studying harder than ever before to do well on their final tests. "Too late for me but you can still save yourself." She looked directly into Ahna's eyes. "It's not too late to give up magic and avoid all this mess."

Ahna laughed at the joke, as Zavala clearly expected her to. "You know," she reminded the older girl, "had you spent a bit more time over the last few years actually studying instead of darting into town every chance you got to meet up with the boys there, you probably wouldn't be as stressed right now."

"True," Zavala admitted with a glint in her eye. "But then it wouldn't have been worth being here at all, now would it?"

The two enjoyed their lunches together with friendly banter. When she was done, Zavala packed her leftovers into the pockets scattered throughout her robes. "Well, I have to go. Don't want to be late to Magi Cornelius's spirit communication class, now do I?" Without waiting for an answer, she stepped up onto the railing, took two steps further out onto the walkway, and jumped over.

The first time Ahna had seen her perform that particular feat, she had run to the edge in a panic, confused as to why the older girl would do something so rash. She had learned immediately that Zavala was an expert flier, able to glide through the air like a bird on the wing. Now, Zavvie's antics no longer caused her panic but it was still amusing when Zavala jumped in front of first-year students, who reacted exactly the same way Ahna herself had.

Not for the first time, Ahna wondered how often Zavala did things like that purely for the shock value. Utterly unafraid to speak her mind, the older student was constantly in trouble for her never-ending stream of pranks. She was definitely jealous of her friend's ability to fly; Ahna herself hadn't been able to do much more than float a few inches off the ground and even that had only lasted for the briefest of moments before gravity had taken hold to reassert its dominance. Now, the closest she got to flight was sitting on her favorite bench, high in the air and looking down as the clouds passed below.

Classes that afternoon were no more exciting than the morning's lectures had been. Elemental manipulation was fine, even though Ahna had no intention of being an Elementalist. While she could see the appeal and usefulness of being able to manipulate the four basic elements of earth, air, fire and water; it simply didn't appeal to her. Being able to control water could prove useful, particularly when one lived on an island or other coastal areas where controlling the floodpath could prove the difference between life and death for entire towns filled with people, towns that had been built too close to the unpredictable water for safety. While her own hometown was near a river, as most towns were, there were plenty of elementalists already available to maintain the town's safety.

Illusions class was always fun, particularly since it wasn't very challenging. Students in the illusions class were much more studious than those in the mental arts class had been, less willing to challenge the ideas by the instructor. On the one hand, Ahna appreciated not having all of the interruptions to the class caused by people like Kerry, but on the other hand, she wondered whether there may be more to the art than just what was being offered. Objecting opinions weren't always a bad thing, after all, and it opened the door for new and fantastic discoveries. After all, to invent a new spell or to expand an existing ability, one had to be able to see beyond just what was already known and accepted.

When it came to scrying class, however, she ran into an issue.

Scrying was the method of using a sphere of crystal, a bowl of water, or a mirror in order to see another area or person. Usually, Ahna used her scrying class as an opportunity to check in on her family but today the water bowl refused to reveal anything. She tried her mother at first, as always, but the water remained clear. Confused, she attempted to view her father instead, but he refused to appear as well.

"Having difficulty today?" Magi Tourner's voice broke through her concentration. The scrying instructor was possibly the oldest living being Ahna had ever encountered. He had likely once stood taller than even Zavala but he was so hunched with age that he was bent almost in half. Spectacles that were thicker than the plates upon which meals were served in the dining hall rested upon his nose and more than once Ahna had heard other students make jokes at his expense, wondering if the weight of his glasses was what had pulled him in half.

"Yes," she admitted as she looked up from the bowl. "I can't get anyone to show up."

"Scrying is difficult," the instructor explained. "It works better if you try scrying upon a person or place to which you are familiar."

"I know," she nodded. "I'm trying to view my parents." She looked down at the bowl, worried. "This is the first time I haven't been able to check in on them since the first week of class."

Magi Tourner raised an eyebrow. "Your parents should be easy enough to view." He looked at her bowl as well. "It appears your setup is correct. Could they have shielding wards in place?"

Shielding wards were special enchantments placed on an area that were designed to block magic from bypassing it, similar to the way a wall kept out unwanted guests. If someone was both very determined and skilled enough, they could bypass the wards just as a thief could scale a wall but that level of magic was beyond Ahna. "That makes sense," she admitted as she thought about it a bit more. "My parents do value their security."

Magi Tourner nodded. "Perhaps you should select a different subject to view, in that case."

She was still considering her inability to view her parents as she left class that evening. What she had said was true; her parents valued their security. However, while her parents had placed shielding wards all over their villa, Ahna had a charm in her pocket that allowed her to bypass the warding for just such a purpose. The fact that she was unable to view her family, despite having been able to view other people in her hometown, bothered her much more than she had let on in class.

"Hey," Zavala caught up to her and once again interrupted her thoughts. "Are you done with classes for the day?" She took the smaller girl's hands in her own and leaned forward, pressing their foreheads together.

As happy as she was to see the girl, Ahna couldn't quite shake the feelings of concern that had plagued her since her failed scrying attempt. "If you're wanting me to come to town with you," Ahna responded, "I'm not really in the mood tonight." Often when Zavala had invited Ahna on her jaunts into Three Rivers, Ahna would decline with the excuse of her studies or other reasonable explanations but that hadn't stopped Zavala from offering.

"No, I wasn't planning on going to the tavern tonight." Zavala placed a firm hand onto Ahna's shoulder and backed a few inches away, far enough to look into her eyes but close enough so that their shared words wouldn't be easily overheard. "I heard something that I wanted to ask you about."

Curious, Ahna met Zavala's intense gaze. "What did you hear?"

Zavala pulled Ahna into a secluded alcove and lowered her voice conspiratorially. "Are you really the daughter of Count de Melville?"

Count de Melville was the head of a powerful family in the Dracott Empire, two kingdoms to the west of the Inland Empire where Three Rivers Academy was located. The de Melville family controlled vast lands which included farms, orchards, and even a handful of small towns. As a result, the Count de Melville was one of the most widely recognized names in the Dracott Empire but this was the first time Ahna had heard anyone reference him since leaving her homeland.

"What makes you think that?" Ahna chuckled at the older girl. "Sure, we're both from the Dracott Empire but that's a pretty big place. Despite what you may have heard, not all of us are related to each other."

"I know," Zavala admitted, "but I thought I overheard a couple of the Magi discussing it earlier today and wanted to make sure."

Ahna shook her head dismissively but secretly she was dying inside. While all of the students and most of the Magi knew her as Ahna Satton, the rumor Zavala had overheard was absolutely true. Her father had insisted on her being enrolled in the school under an artificial name for both her security and the security of her family, a ploy that had worked flawlessly for three years. Of everyone she knew at the Academy, Zavala was the one student with whom Ahna had desperately wished she could share her secret.

She wondered if there was some connection between her identity being revealed and her inability to reach her family in scrying class and her blood ran cold at the thought. As the heir to a powerful family, she had grown up with the understanding that there was danger lurking around every corner. In fact, that had been one of the main reasons why she had been sent all the way to the Inland Empire to attend the Academy. Her father had decided that she would be much safer in an area where she would not be as easily recognized as she would have been in one of the academies nearer to her home.

Ahna continued to listen quietly as Zavala chattered on but she paid no attention to the older girl. Her mind whirled with possibilities: not only possibilities about her family and why she hadn't been able to contact them, but also possibilities about how her friend had learned of her true identity.

2

The students who learned in and graduated from the hallowed halls of the Three Rivers Academy weren't the only thing in which the Magi and students took pride. There was the long history that enshrouded the building itself, which was widely touted as the oldest and longest-functioning magical learning center in the Inland Empire. That reputation was wholly deserved, as the building had overseen countless students for well over three hundred years. Inbound students were quick to discover that the Academy had once been a small building where a small gathering of Magi had come together to share knowledge amongst themselves in order to teach their students a wider variety of abilities than any of them could be taught individually. In the years since, it had only grown, both in size and in depth and breadth of skills learned.

For those seeking a more visual experience of the Academy's history, the portrait gallery was a draw. It held portraits of every distinguishing alumnus from the Academy, many of whom had become famous throughout the world for their talents. The oldest were of the founding Magi, small drawings made by their students to honor the instructors. Every year, new portraits were added to the gallery as Magi reached the esteemed status of instructor, the only position deemed worthy of a place of honor among the hanging portraits.

Others may choose to view the gardens, a beautiful and colorful landscape that was constantly stocked and maintained with the common varieties of herbs and flowers used in the base levels of magic. First year students were selected to maintain the gardens, an honor nobody took lightly. Among the hyssop and geranium, small pockets of more powerful herbs could be found, planted by advanced students and tended rigorously. Each student was allowed to add one type of plant to the gardens, or to expand an existing type of plant by one bed. As a result, the potionmakers had an almost-endless supply of these ingredients. Small insects were commonplace among the gardens, their presence encouraged to increase plant growth and were used occasionally as a supply for some concoctions themselves.

The peak of the southernmost tower soared high above the clouds and offered an unparalleled view of the entire landscape, unrestricted by the surrounding buildings. By standing on the top floor of the tower on a clear day, even the island of Hub could be seen. Rumors told of flying beasts that arrived and left by use of the platform on the southern tower, rumors that held far more truth than exaggeration. Truth in those rumors could be found by the myriad scratches and gouges across the topmost floor of the tower, evidence of large animals landing there and scrabbling for grip on the stone and wood floors. What, precisely, had been those flying creatures was still a highly contested debate among students.

But almost unanimously, the biggest source of pride was the library.

The Three Rivers Academy library took up three entire floors of one of the towers, with wood-paneled walls and carved frescoes scattered throughout the beams. Light shone in from the windows that surrounded it, some of which were clear while some were covered with ornate patterns of stained glass in a rainbow of hues, causing dappled light shows across the study tables as the sun traveled on its leisurely journey across the sky. Tables, benches, desks, sofas, and armchairs were scattered everywhere, granting even the most ancient of bones a comfortable place to rest, read, or study. Spiral staircases carved of deep ebony wood were placed evenly around all three stories of the library, each granting easy access to all three levels. Deep within a row of bookshelves on the lowermost level, Ahna sighed.

"*Fifteen Uses for Chupacabra Blood*," she read the title of the book and decided that it was not what she was looking for. "*Theories on Trolls and Regeneration. Water Magic from the Merfolk. Simple Charms for Students. Preserving Snow for More Potent Ice Magic.*" None of the books in this section of the library appeared to have what she was looking for. "Where are all the books on which components to use for scrying rituals?"

Rituals were more powerful versions of the

regular spells most students were studying. After her failure in scrying class the previous day, she had decided to try the stronger ritual in order to try making contact with her parents, just to be sure that they were okay. While she hoped that someone would notify her if something bad had happened, sometimes information didn't move as quickly as everyone would like. Particularly when one was as far away from home as she currently was. She dismissed the thoughts immediately, before they had a chance to burrow into her subconscious and fester. Even as far away from home as she was, there were ample opportunities and means for a messenger to get word to her should something befall her family. The fact that word had not been delivered was information in and of itself.

"As the saying goes," she reminded herself, "no news is good news."

As she walked down the length of the aisle, searching every book title on the shelves, a quiet conversation on the next aisle caught her attention.

"You can't be serious," a voice said in hushed

tones. "Why would the Grand Coven recruit you?" Doubt was evident in the speaker's voice.

"I have no idea," another voice replied. "But she said they were looking for people with remarkable power and I made the list."

"But is that even a list you want to be on? I mean, even if they really are recruiting you, that sounds like a bad life choice to me."

"Why? If a powerful group was recruiting you, you'd be eager to get aboard."

"Not if it was the Grand Coven recruiting me, I wouldn't. That's practically signing your own death warrant if you get caught!"

"Nah," the mystery voice laughed. "I think you're just jealous because they contacted me and not you."

Both voices faded away as the speakers moved toward the stairs, leaving Ahna in quiet solitude once more. She stood motionless until she was certain that both speakers had left the area before slipping the book she had been holding back onto the shelf where it belonged. "What is the Grand Coven doing in Three Rivers?" This far away from home, she hadn't expected to even hear of the group, let alone find them recruiting new members. The safety and security offered to her by the location and reputation of the Academy was suddenly much less assured than it had been only moments before.

Thoroughly distracted by the conversation she had overheard, Ahna grabbed an assortment of books from the next shelf in the row without paying much attention to the topics covered by each and headed toward one of the sitting areas to scan through them. She was less interested in what information the books had to offer but it was the best way she could think of to get herself back into her research and her mind back on track. Had her need to contact her family been any less, she may have abandoned the search altogether but family bonds outweighed unsubstantiated rumors. Despite her intention to focus on communication with her family, her mind soon returned to the overheard conversation about the Grand Coven.

Although she couldn't say for certain, a part of Ahna wondered if the Grand Coven played a part in her parents' decision to send her to learn in Three Rivers. Although they were never spoken of openly, there had been plenty of rumors about the Coven back in her hometown of Ruschlack.

Neither of her parents put any stock in the rumor mill and Ahna couldn't count how many times she had been admonished to make decisions based on facts instead of supposition, to pay more attention to things that were real and less to things that were imaginary. For those same people who had taught her to remain firmly rooted to the ground in all aspects of her life to speak quietly of the Coven strongly indicated that the mysterious group was more fact than rumor. Ahna herself had once accidentally overheard a conversation between her mother and father on the topic.

Just over four years previously, before she had even heard of Three Rivers and the Academy she now attended, she spent most of her afternoons playing in the field between her house and the woods that surrounded Ruschlack Lake and picking wildflowers with her little brother. That was a normal occurrence for them, as Ahna loved seeing each type of flower and how they each changed during their life cycles and her brother had loved the scents and colors offered by each. She had come back indoors to grab a vase to put their collection of blooms into when she overheard her parents talking. From the upper landing, she had overheard them discussing events that hadn't made sense to her at the time but became clearer as she had learned more about the world. At the time the overheard conversation had taken place, she hadn't yet discovered what a necromancer was but, according to her father, one had been in Tomens, the capital city of the Dracott Empire, only days previously.

"They're calling soldiers in from across the Empire," father had explained. "From what I understand, the undead are still flooding the area."

At first, Ahna had believed that her father was simply making jokes to her mother, as that was the only context she had held for tales of the undead. Children often told stories to frighten their friends, fantastic tales about hordes of skeletal creatures, many composed of human remains but often including those from other beasts as well. She had ceased to believe in the possibility long ago, feeling far too old and mature even at the young age she was to believe in such horror stories any longer.

"My gods," mother had replied. "Do they know where they came from?"

"Necromancer, most certainly." He continued

to explain that some of the local lords appeared to believe the death mage was a part of a group known as the Grand Coven, sent to exterminate a large portion of the Dracott Empire's defensive forces. "We think this might be the first wave of a larger invasion, so we are sending in more troops to combat the undead and for more magical defenses to bolster what we already have."

As he spoke, Ahna grew more alarmed at the news. The more he explained of the situation, the less Ahna believed the conversation to be a joke played upon her mother. Had he been aware that his daughter lurked nearby, her father would likely have not explained nearly as much as he had. His words had been frightening to his wife and particularly more so when overheard by a small child.

Tomens, seat of the Empire and home of Emperor du Toit, had some of the strongest defenses in the entire Dracott Empire, both magical and mundane. The emperor's guard, practically a standing military in its own right, was formed of the most skillful and powerful warriors across the empire, many of whom had been trained in the magical arts to bolster their fighting skills. There was even rumor, proof of which Ahna had never seen but had plenty of reasons to believe, of hidden weapons built into buildings, purchased at no small price from the impressively skilled smiths from a town located within the Inland Empire called Greystone.

Ahna was still lost in her memories as she carried the stack of books back to her chambers. Although she hadn't personally seen the aftermath of the necromancer's assault on Tomens, she had heard plenty about it. Over half of the emperor's personal guard had been killed, many of whom had been raised back to life by the evil wizard of death to join the fight against their own comrades. Portions of the city had been reduced to so much rubble, despite the Greystone-created defenses, and many of its terrified inhabitants had fled the area, more than a few of whom found themselves settling in Ruschlack. Although she had heard the initial news from her father, it had been from the survivors that Ahna had heard the true level of horror they had experienced, the nightmares that continued to haunt them of watching their friends and loved ones being brought back to a state of undeath.

It had taken less than a year after the assault for Ahna to be sent to Three Rivers.

"Whoa," a familiar voice broke through her memories. "Looks like you've got something pretty massive on your mind."

The memories faded and she found herself back in familiar hallways, outside the door of her own chambers, where Zavala had been waiting for her return. "What do you know about the Grand Coven?" she asked as she led her into her rooms.

"The Grand Coven?" Zavala followed her inside and closed the door behind them. "Why are you asking about them?"

"I overheard a conversation in the library today." Ahna set the books down on her desk and reached over to open the curtains to let more light into the room. "It sounded like students were being recruited."

Zavala laughed. "I'm not surprised." In response to Ahna's expression of shock, she explained. "Every year, some of the older students tell the younger students about this super dark and scary group that is hunting magic users." She lowered her voice conspiratorially as she told the tale.

"Legend says that there is an ancient group of

powerful Magi known as the Grand Coven. Its members know all of the secrets of magic and have in their possession the most powerful spells and rituals, even ones that have been lost to the history of time. To maintain their control over the use of magic, they watch over the magical activity across all of the empires, finding those who seem to have exceptional talent and power. Those people they watch over to determine how much use they will have to the Coven. Once they are deemed worthy, the Grand Coven will send someone to meet with these people to either recruit them or, if they refuse, to kill them."

"That's terrible!" Ahna exclaimed. "Why don't the Magi do something to stop them?"

"Because," Zavala dropped her voice further until it was barely above a whisper, "many of the Magi throughout the Academy are actually members of the Grand Coven. They were placed here and in all of the other magical training academies to watch for young, talented students that they can then groom into joining the Coven.

"It's even said that some members of the Coven are older than recorded history and that's how they know so much about ancient, forgotten magic. They know the secrets of eternal life and eternal youth. Some say that there are even have a handful of members who have been dead for hundreds of years and yet continue to maintain their power and knowledge, with every appearance of life unless you know their deep, dark secrets."

Ahna sank into a chair, her eyes wide in shock. She had thought that by coming all the way to the Inland Sea she would be safe from the Grand Coven, only now to discover that she was surrounded by them. How could she have not realized the danger she had been in until now? Why would her father have sent her to this place, so far from home, if she wasn't safe? "Why didn't you tell me about this before?" she demanded of her friend. "We've been friends for years, why didn't you say something about all this if you knew about it?"

"Because it's not real. It's just a horror tale meant to frighten new students. There is no such thing as the Grand Coven and the Magi aren't planning to kill you if you get too powerful." She sat on the arm of Ahna's chair and put a comforting arm around her, blue feathers and brown hair tickling her ear in the process. "So, you see, there was nothing to warn you about in the first place."

After taking a moment to consider her friend's words, Ahna accepted that Zavala really didn't know the truth. This far away from the Dracott Empire, the likelihood that the Grand Coven had as much influence as the legend Zavala had revealed was very little indeed. If the stories of the Grand Coven were no more than horror tales, Ahna decided not to reveal her personal knowledge otherwise. There was no reason to spark the kind of fear that she knew would be forthcoming if Zavala knew the truth.

"But," Zavala eyed her critically, "if there was such a thing, do you think you'd want to join up?"

"Why would I want to do that?" The very idea sent a shudder down her spine.

"Oh, there are plenty of reasons." Zavala settled into a chair. "Eternal life, for one. Imagine never growing old and becoming dependent on your children for your survival; being always young and full of possibilities. Riches beyond compare. Power and prestige. The ability to control entire towns, entire empires, with nobody to stop you. That's the stuff dreams are made of, things people have been fighting for since time began."

Ahna shook her head, eyes lowered. "I don't

think I need all that," she said. "I just want a quiet life where I can use my magic to make people happy. Maybe even help them, if I can." She had seen far too much suffering in her homeland to ever wish that kind of pain on anyone.

3

Ahna spent the next couple weeks primarily in the library, partly due to her class studies and partly to see what she could find on the Grand Coven, particularly in regards to their presence in the Inland Empire. Considering how prevalent Zavala had said that the legend of the Grand Coven was throughout the Academy, Ahna had expected to find at least some reference to it in one of the books on the Academy's history but after days of searching she had to admit defeat. There was simply no mention of the apparently secretive group to be found.

"No big surprise," she remarked to herself. "Secret groups don't often go around advertising their presence. At least, not if they want to stay secret for any length of time."

After her fifth consecutive day finding nothing, she considered asking one of the omnipresent librarians for assistance but decided against it. Even if Zavala had been correct that most people assumed the Coven's existence to be nothing more than a tall tale, Ahna had no interest in gaining the attention of any of the Magi in her search. With all of the books in the great library, there just had to be something of use to her. She only needed to find it.

Not for the first time, her gaze fell to the one area of the library to which she, as with all students of the Academy, had been denied access. The restricted area was for Magi and visiting loremasters and sages only. Even those esteemed visitors were only allowed access to specific books and scrolls within the restricted section and were always closely supervised. Even that level of access was entirely dependent upon having their request granted by the Magi, few of which were approved. Given what she already knew about the dangers inherent in the Grand Coven, if there was any information about them to be had, it would be in there.

From the outside, the restricted area appeared

to be nothing more than a black iron door covered with etchings of arcane runes. From what she could identify from what few classes she had taken on the matter, some of the runes were simple enough: basic wards against scrying, teleportation, telepathic communication and any other means of viewing or accessing things without the proper permissions. Those levels of protection were more than enough to secure the room against all but the most determined of curious onlookers. She doubted that the runes she had been able to identify were the entirety of defenses for the room, otherwise higher-level students would have gained access to it ages ago.

"If there's one thing that will drive people bonkers," she mused to her pages of notes, "it is to be denied access." Regardless of the value of the items stored behind the iron barrier, anything that wasn't general knowledge was assumed to be behind the vault door. Every student had heard tales of one previous student or another who attempted to gain unlawful entry only to be thwarted by the room's defenses. Worse, any who were caught breaking in were immediately censured, some even evicted from the Academy's grounds, their tenure as students negated by the single act of defiance.

Additionally, Ahna wasn't even certain of how large the restricted section was. From the outside it only appeared to be a few feet wide and barely further than that deep, but even the most novice of magical students knew that appearances could be deceiving. While she didn't know how to perform the magic herself, Ahna was aware of a ritual that could expand the interior space of an area by multiples of its original capacity, so that small room could easily be the size of the rest of the library beyond the door. The ritual was taught to third-year students and while she had considered taking the course, it didn't fit with her current curriculum.

Less likely, she realized, was the possibility that there was simply no information on the Grand Coven to be found in the Academy library. Given the distance between the Inland and Dracott Empires, it was entirely possible that even had the Coven expanded its area of influence to the Inland Empire, the Coven hadn't gotten much of a foothold in the area yet. She found that possibility to be highly unlikely, however, due to the legends passed from senior students to the more innocent beginners. Even if it was just campfire lore in the Inland Empire, the mere knowledge of the Grand Coven should have been enough for someone to feel the need to do further research in the origins of the tales.

It could also be the case, she realized, that the Academy had indeed been infiltrated by members of the Coven, mages who were so intent on keeping their activities secret that they removed or destroyed any mention of the group from the grounds. The more she considered the idea, the more plausible it sounded. Not so much in the infiltration of the Academy but more so in the Coven going to great lengths to keep themselves from being easily researched. "If I was a member of something like that," she shuddered at the thought, "I certainly wouldn't want anyone to uncover information about it." She pulled over another piece of paper, determined to begin making notes on what she already knew about the group just in case there was some sort of conspiracy afoot.

As though hearing her thoughts, one of the librarians came to see her. "Magi Andress wants to see you in his office." He adjusted his spectacles, which covered almost half of his face, as he spoke.

Confused by the request and surprised by the interruption, Ahna left the books she had been perusing on the table where she had been studying. Students often had to leave their study materials for periods of time and they were usually still there when they returned, so long as they returned the same day. Overnight, library staff gathered all of the abandoned materials and replaced them onto their appropriate shelves, whether by manual labor or automatic enchantment, nobody knew. Wondering if the summons to Magi Andress's office had anything to do with her search for information on the Grand Coven, she was a little concerned about what was in store for her when she arrived. Her interest in the mysterious group couldn't possibly be reason for her to come under the watchful eyes of the Magi, could it? Or had she inadvertently broken some other taboo, something of which she had been unaware?

Magi Andress's office was compact and slightly crowded. A low fire flickered in yellow, orange, and red flames in the fireplace, which was surrounded by evenly-sized stone panels in varying shades of brown. The mantle held a small series of books with unreadable spines, an inkwell with the tip of a long brown and cream-colored quill resting inside it, and an assortment of bottles and jars that contained items Ahna didn't want to consider. Rows of bookshelves lined two of the office walls, interrupted only by a pair of brass candle sconces that jutted out from the wall between stacks of books. A stack of dirty gray boxes with worn rope handles stood against a third wall near the door and Magi Andress's desk waited in the center of the room. His desk was littered with papers, an unlit lantern, opened books, and a handful of other items that Ahna couldn't identify without closer inspection. The Magi himself sat behind the desk, carefully perusing one of the loose sheets of paper.

"You requested me?" Since the Magi had obviously not noticed her arrival, Ahna didn't want to startle the man but there was no telling how long it would take for him to look away from his work.

Magi Andress was elderly, as many of the instructors at the Academy were, with wavy hair that still contained some of the sandy blond he had once owned. Large round glasses rested upon his nose, framing light brown eyes. Unlike the other instructors Ahna had encountered, Magi Andress was not wearing his robes, although she could see them hanging from a hook behind his door. Instead, he was wearing a knitted cream-colored sweater with buttons at the collar and a pair of green-brown pants.

"Yes, Ahna." He placed the paper he had been reading aside, facing down so that any lettering on the page would not be visible to a casual observer. "Please, have a seat."

Ahna sat in the ancient leather chair opposite him, still curious as to the nature of her visit to his office. From his demeanor, it didn't appear that she was in trouble of any sort but she couldn't imagine any other reason for a student to be called in to speak with one of the administrators. Rather than asking directly, however, she waited patiently for him to explain his reasons.

"It's about your father," he explained once she was seated. "I'm afraid there's no easy way to explain this; we've just received word that he has been killed."

Ahna felt the blood drain from her face as he spoke but she heard nothing beyond that first sentence. She could see that Magi Andress continued to speak for a beat or two further but none of the sounds he made reached her ears. The ground wobbled beneath her feet and she was thankful that she was seated, else she knew she would have fallen to the floor most ungracefully.

Although a part of her had suspected that the reason she had been unable to contact her father was because he wasn't around to contact any longer, she hadn't allowed herself to seriously entertain the possibility. Why had it taken so long for someone to send word to her? Her mother, she was certain, was beside herself with the news. Finally, she shook a question from the clouds that filled her mind. "What happened?"

"We aren't entirely certain yet, as we have only received minimal information so far, but it appears he was assassinated."

Even though she had entertained the idea that her father could have died, she hadn't even considered the possibility of it having been deliberate. If anything, she had suspected an accident or an illness, never murder. "Do you know who did it? Or who ordered it?" Perhaps that was why extra warding had been placed around the family, warding strong enough that even Ahna's bypass charm couldn't penetrate. When he shook his head in response, she changed her line of questioning. "What about my mother? My brother? Are they safe?"

"I don't know," he admitted. "The only information I have is on your father but we have been trying to contact the rest of your family and have so far been unable to do so. I understand from Magi Tourner that you have recently experienced the same results with your attempts to contact them via scrying. Much as we all hope that they are safe, until we are able to make contact with someone to determine otherwise, I think it's best to act under the assumption that they are gone as well."

The more powerful a person or family was, the more likely they would be targeted for personal, political, or financial gain. That understanding was why Count de Melville valued security so much and why he had his own personal guard for his household. However, no matter how strong one's guard was, there was always a weak point where someone determined enough could slip through to do damage.

It was because of this threat that all members of the de Melville family had marks placed upon their bodies. These marks were intended to protect them from various forms of elemental damage, particularly fire, and to generate a level of shielding against direct or magical attacks. Ahna herself had such markings upon her body, ink placed beneath the skin to form an intricate pattern of sigils across her back. They had been placed upon her only days after she had been born, as they had been for every generation born into the de Melville family since they had first become targets for assassination, even those who married into the family received the same markings. The sigils they had served the family well for more generations than Ahna could count in protecting against most would-be killers. Ahna had received one additional mark to the pattern before leaving for the Academy, a special sigil that allowed her to bypass the defenses of her family in order to contact them while she was away even if she lost her bypass charm. A sigil which had proven to be useless after all. With no family remaining to contact, scrying would be pointless and a bypass charm did nothing for contacting those who had already passed from this life.

Even with all of the family markings, someone

had managed to assassinate her father. The thought chilled her to the bone. Who could have done such a thing? Her whole lineage depended on the sigils for protection and none so far had managed to circumvent that protection to land a direct assault on her family. Whoever had managed to kill her father must be either a powerful magus, the likes of which she had heard only in legend, or the most skilled assassin the world had ever known.

"You will be protected while you are here," Magi Andress continued. "The Academy puts the safety of our students as one of our highest priorities, so there should be very little risk to you, particularly since only a couple of the Magi know your true identity. I understand that you were instructed similarly upon your arrival but I feel I must stress once again the importance of not revealing yourself to anyone here. The fewer who know who you truly are, the more effectively we can keep you safe."

The Magi continued to talk but Ahna no longer heard his words. She had already agreed to stay within the halls of the Academy during her stay and, despite numerous invitations from Zavala and other friends, she had not yet ventured beyond its walls so further reminders to stay within the safety of its towers were pointless. Also pointless was Magi Andress's assurance that nobody outside a handful of senior Magi knew of her identity; Zavala's questions on Ahna's relationship to the Count had already proven otherwise. She had no way to know how widespread the knowledge had gone, despite her denials to Zavala. Words spoken by one, her father had been prone to say, were words known by many.

She didn't need more guards to watch over her on the Academy grounds. She didn't need more sigils embedded in her skin to protect her against unseen attacks. She didn't need to go to the taverns with her friends to sample exotic wines. She didn't even need the familiar companionship of Zavala. All Ahna needed at that very moment was to go to bed, pull the covers up over her face, and fall asleep in the hopes that she would wake in the morning and discover that all of this had been nothing more than a very bad dream.

She walked in a daze to her rooms, much like the period between sleep and wakefulness where it is unclear whether walking in a dream or reality. If she could only wake from this dream, the world would be the one she always knew. She could hear her father's voice again. She could smell the clean, slightly rose-scented air that her mother left behind whenever she moved through a room. She could experience the frustration of one of her brother's endless, insignificant pranks that he loved to play upon her. Other students passed by her in the hallways as she walked, some laughing and carrying on as though the world somehow continued for everyone but her. A small voice in the back of her mind rose up against the good humor that surrounded her, infuriated those other students dared to be in such high spirits. She quickly tamped down on the feelings, recognizing that they weren't real, or at least that they weren't a real reflection of how she felt.

Every fiber of her being wished with all of her might that this was nothing more than the single worst nightmare she had ever experienced, despite knowing at her core that it was nothing as simple as that. No nightmare could cause the feeling of abject helplessness she now experienced, the absolute loneliness of knowing her family was gone. Her mother would never walk through the halls, her father had no more words of wisdom to offer. Her brother's stream of pranks and foolery had ended, along with the entire world she had once known.

The halls felt alien, as though she didn't belong within them, orphaned as she now was. These halls were intended for those whose families loved them and eagerly awaited their return. For those who still had joy enough to laugh freely among themselves. Once her training was complete, she no longer had a home to return to. Sure, the manor would still stand and the staff would maintain everything as though the Count was still alive, but a manor without her family would never again be a home.

Head held high, not a single tear fell before she was safely closed within the private walls of her own rooms. No matter what manner of hard times had befallen them, a de Melville never showed weakness in public.

Her father insisted.

4

The administrators of the Academy had made good on Magi Andress's promise of additional security, Ahna noted over the next few days. It seemed like she could hardly go anywhere on campus without seeing Magi. Alarm sigils had been placed throughout the floors she frequented, as had additional sigils to reduce elemental damage. The halls leading to her rooms were lined with alternating sigils, each of which was intended to protect against all manner of accidental and intentional dangers. Given the amount of extra security that appeared to be centered around her and the areas she frequented, Ahna wondered how long it would take for people to realize that she was the cause.

She had been granted a leave of absence from

her classes for the week after being told of her father's death, time of which she spent the majority in the library. After only a few days, the desk she regularly piled with books and notes had become known as her area and all of the librarians took care to keep others away, granting her the space she so obviously needed. She didn't need the space for the reasons everyone believed, however. There was nothing in the library that would undo what had been done to her family.

No longer researching rituals to contact her parents, she spent the time looking through information on sigils, particularly those found on her own body. Although she knew generally what they were used for, she had only identified a handful of them. After a couple of hours before the mirror in her dressing room, she had made a copy of the entire glyph, hopefully without too many errors. If her family had indeed been murdered, she needed to know to what types of magic and other forms of damage she was resistant and to what, by process of elimination, she was vulnerable. "Preparation is key," she reminded herself, yet another favorite phrase of her father's.

Although she had no reason to believe that

whatever had befallen her family would follow her to Three Rivers, she was now the last living person among her immediate relatives, automatic scion of the de Melville family. There were a great many things that she would need to understand in order to take over her family's estates, most of which had been information held in reserve for her return after graduation. That timeline had been shortened drastically by this latest turn of events and, although she didn't have all of the information she would eventually need at hand, she could at the very least determine what she could from her current position. When she returned home, there would be much waiting for her, demanding her attention, so the better prepared she was for it, the easier she would be able to navigate it all.

She confirmed that she was resistant to most forms of elemental magic, specifically fire, water, air, and earth. Additionally, she was resistant to lightning damage and darkness-based damage, which surprised her. While lightning magic was uncommon but not unheard-of, she had never encountered even the barest mention of darkness magic and hadn't the slightest idea why she would need protection against it.

"Maybe that's connected to necromancy," she mused to herself as she perused through yet another book on protective sigils. "Necromancy is supposed to be one of the darkest types of magic, so perhaps by protecting against darkness, this sigil also protects against necromancy." Not finding what she was looking for, she changed sections and went in search of information about necromancy. Even if her assumption about the connection between the sigil and necromantic magic was mistaken, she was still interested in knowing more.

Necromancy, more commonly referred to as death magic, was banned in many areas, including the Dracott Empire. While it didn't appear to be banned in the Inland Empire, it wasn't taught in the Academy, at least as far as Ahna could tell with a cursory glance. She was surprised to see books on the topic available on the shelves. She had expected that even if the Academy had books on necromancy, they would have been stored in the restricted area.

Practitioners of necromancy were reportedly able to raise the dead back to life, under the mage's control, such as those used to attack Tomens all those years ago. A creeping sensation crawled down her spine at the memory, a sensation which she brushed aside. There was no time to dawdle on reflections of a past long since gone.

Additionally, they could communicate with the dead, both those recently passed and those who had been gone for much longer. Necromantic magic could cause damage not just to the body, which was possible with almost all forms of elemental magic, but it could also cause damage to the soul itself and heal damage caused to the soul as well. By combining this soul repair ability with the ability to communicate with the dead, some necromancers were even able to restore the soul of a deceased person back into a healed body, effectively resurrecting the dead similarly to the way a powerful cleric may be able.

"So maybe necromancers are less about death itself but more about the connection between life and death," she wondered as she set the book aside and reached for another. "Apparently it's not all about reanimating dead bodies, if they can actually bring one back to life as well." She made a mental note on the idea, deciding that it would require more thought later. Most of the information she had already learned about necromancy had come from horror stories from the Tomens refugees, so now she wondered whether all necromancers were as destructive as those ones had been. If there was benefit to the necromantic arts, perhaps there was bias to it as well.

As with all students, Ahna had been required to take an introduction to magic course during her first year. During that class, one of the topics that had been covered was the perceived difference between so-called "light" and "dark" magic. The instructor had demonstrated, using a basic levitation spell as an example, how perception gave meaning to light and dark magic. He levitated one of the students a few inches off the ground. "By my levitation of this student," he asked the class, "is this an indication of good or evil?"

The class had generally agreed that levitation did not appear to be a harmful spell, so it was probably okay to use, therefore "light" magic.

"But what if I used this same spell to levitate this student over a high cliff?" he asked. "What if I released the spell, dropping him from that same cliff? Would it still be a good spell? Would you still consider it to be "light" magic then?"

The students decided that they had initially been mistaken, by using the spell to cause harm to the student, that made it dark magic.

"People view things they do not understand as evil and evil things are automatically dark," the instructor had explained. "But magic does not know good or evil, it is simply focused intent towards a goal. Therefore, magic itself cannot be good and cannot be evil. That effect is entirely determined by the intent of the mage." He gently lowered the student to the floor, much to the student's relief. Even though there were no steep cliffs in the classroom, the idea had caused a thin sheen of sweat to appear across his face.

"Perhaps the same concept applies to necromancy," Ahna considered. The only personal reference she had to that type of magic had been the devastation of Tomens and its residents but if there was the capacity for much good to be done with necromantic spells, perhaps she had simply been naïve. Although she couldn't think of a good reason to raise the dead back to life as mindless skeletal warriors, she had to admit that the ability to repair damage to the soul could be a good thing. After all, mages who used too much power too quickly, or who tried abilities that were outside of their power level, ran the risk of damaging their own souls as a result.

"Why are you looking at necromancy?" Zavala asked as she sat down next to Ahna. "I thought you were specializing in mental magic."

"I am," she replied, "at least for now. But I came across these while I was looking up sigils and got curious."

"Well, if you're worried about necromancers, I wouldn't be too concerned. There aren't any near here." Zavala flashed her patented grin towards her friend, tucked a feather behind her ear, and changed the subject. "You've been cooped up in here for far too long. There's a new trading center that just opened not too far from here. Word is that the witch who runs the place has lots of odd-ball stuff and all the components you could ever want for really cheap. Some of us are heading up to check it out. You should come with us."

Although the outing sounded interesting, Ahna hadn't forgotten Magi Andress's warning to remain within the Academy's protection. "Maybe another time."

Ahna stood firm as Zavala tried to argue. "You

know," the older girl said as she stood up to leave, "this isn't a prison. You act like you can't ever go out and do anything fun but you aren't a prisoner here." It was a common argument when Zavala really wanted Ahna to join her on an outing but, as usual, Ahna remained behind while her friend went out to explore.

She returned to her original research into sigils, putting necromancy aside in her mind for the time being. As far as she was concerned, there would be plenty of time later for her to research that topic further. She didn't get very deep into her reading before her attention drifted once again to a nearby conversation.

"It sounds like things are moving towards a war for power," one student explained, "so they're looking for mages to come out and help keep the peace."

"Who's trying to start a war?" another student asked.

"More importantly," a third student interrupted, "how much are they offering to pay us?" Of the three students, Kerry was the only one whose voice Ahna recognized.

"They need to find someone to take the throne next and just about everyone wants it."

"Won't it just go to the emperor's son?"

The first student shook his head. "Dracott doesn't do things that way. Their throne doesn't always stay within the same family, it goes to whoever the emperor picks as his successor."

"So what's wrong with the guy he picked?"

"And what about the money? I'll go help keep the peace if the payment's right."

"Dead. Killed by Dark Star is what I heard."

By the time the conversation reached that point, Ahna already knew they were discussing her father. Even though Count de Melville's selection as the next emperor was supposed to be a guarded secret, apparently that secrecy hadn't extended to the students of the Academy. She was surprised to hear it being discussed openly among the three students; others in the school were bound to know about it as well. She had to wonder just how many supposed secrets were general knowledge among the students.

More so, the mention of Dark Star gave her pause. She knew the name, of course, every lord and lady in the Dracott Empire knew of the legendary assassin. Although he had only been known to operate in the empire for fewer than ten years, it was generally assumed that many deaths that had occurred in that time had been the result of his actions. Nobody seemed to know from where he had come, nor his true identity. The only things that were known was that he could kill with an airborne dagger at a hundred paces, that he carried a pair of specialty hooked swords, and that he would never kill a child, regardless of the payment offered.

"Not just that," the students continued discussing, "but he didn't just kill the Count, he killed his entire family. Wife, son, all of 'em."

"I thought he had a girl, too. What happened to her?"

"I thought she died a long time ago. At least, nobody's seen her in years."

"Maybe she was the first," Kerry offered. "Kill the daughter as a warning so the Count does what Dark Star wants. The Count doesn't do what he says he's gonna do, he takes out the rest of the family."

"That's not how assassins work," the first student interjected. "Assassins are just tools, sent by other people who hire them just like any other laborer."

"So what? That just means that whoever hired the Dark Star has the demands that weren't met. Doesn't exactly change the outcome, now does it?"

"Not in the slightest," Kerry chuckled. "No matter how you look at it, dead is dead."

Even had it not been for a lifetime of her parents teaching her to ignore rumors and hearsay, Ahna would still have stopped paying much attention at that point. At first, she thought that perhaps Kerry and her friends had heard news that she had been unaware of but what they were saying didn't make much sense. Although Ahna herself was also suspicious that her father hadn't been the only victim of the assassin, the details of the rumors she was overhearing didn't sound quite correct. Firstly, she knew that the Dark Star, while dangerous, never killed children, so there was no way he would have killed her brother. Pretty much everyone in the Dracott Empire knew better than to try hiring him to kill a child, the person seeking the assassination was more likely to be killed than the target. Secondly, she knew for an absolute fact that the Count's daughter had not been killed as a warning to her father.

Unless, at ten years of age, her brother was no longer under whatever age threshold the assassin used to decide whether someone was too young to be targeted. Not for the first time, she wondered why Dark Star refused to kill children, or at what age they stopped being considered children in his eyes.

"Rubbish," she grumbled to herself as she returned to her books. She needed to stop musing on an assassin that was more fiction than fact and start focusing on her actual research. While she was pleased that her identity hadn't become general knowledge, hearing whispered news of her own death was more distressing than she had expected. She thought of the friends she had known back home. Did they think she was dead as well?

One piece of rumor the students had gotten correct, she had to admit, was that Count de Melville had been expected to take over rulership of the Dracott Empire when Emperor du Toit passed. While the emperor's health continued to fail, despite the quantity of healers that were no doubt in attendance, there was no longer anyone who had been prepared to take the throne upon the event of his death.

5

Despite the conversation Ahna overheard in the library, discussions on events in the Dracott Empire, particularly those surrounding the death of Count de Melville, were not as widespread a topic of conversation throughout the Academy as she had initially feared. The following day she would be required to attend classes once again and she didn't want to spend her remaining free time focused on idle gossip. Still unable to contact her mother or brother, she had accepted the likelihood that they had indeed been killed alongside her father, a thought which gave her no small amount of concern.

She still had a few years left of study at the Academy before she was expected to return home as a fully accredited magus in her own right but suddenly becoming the last remaining member of her family demanded that she consider changing her expectations. She doubted that she would be able to remain in Three Rivers for much longer, as there were many people who relied on her family for guidance and stability. Without the family in place to make the decisions that impacted the landholders, there would certainly be problems aplenty waiting for her when she returned home. She needed to come up with a plan and she needed to do it quickly.

If there was only some means by which she could appoint someone to oversee things until she finished her education, that would make her situation much easier. Historically there had been times where similar actions had been taken, in fact her father had once stood in place of the emperor while Emperor du Toit had been called for business in other lands. However, as she considered who may be available to oversee the de Melville estate for the upcoming years, she couldn't help but wonder if any of the viable options could be trusted.

After all, someone had killed her father. It was highly unlikely that the killer had been of the nobles waiting for their chance to take his place in line for the crown, as that would require proximity and a level of daring that she doubted many of them possessed. It was, however, not only possible but probable that one of them had arranged for it. Worse, she realized, it may not have been just one person who wanted her family dead. It could easily have been a pact among multiple members of the Dracott Empire hierarchy. Just because she and other members of her family viewed their actions as benevolent and for the good of all, that viewpoint wasn't automatically shared among everyone who answered to them. It wouldn't be the first time lower-ranking families had banded together to seize control from those above.

A chill ran down her spine as she recalled the conversation overheard in the library. There were already other families vying for the throne only days after the news of her father's death. In order for so many of them to be prepared to go to such lengths, at least some of them must have already been aware the assassination would happen. She thought of all the events she had attended at the estates of other noble Dracott Empire households, wondering how many heads of household had been scheming, plotting behind their backs, and for how long. Would the same fate befall her, she wondered, when she returned home? Would any of her protective sigils save her from the same fate as her family? The sigils hadn't done much to save other members of her family, after all.

She sat at her desk with her thoughts, a sheaf of loose paper, and a cup of floral tea that Zavala had brought back from her exploration of Dragon Keep, the most recent exploration that Ahna had refused to join her on. The tea was supposed to calm and soothe, which Ahna appreciated. Although she had tried to hide her upset over the last few days, her observant friend had obviously realized something was wrong. Given their previous conversation about Ahna's relationship to the de Melville family and the more recent news of the Count's death, it stood to reason that Zavala had put the pieces together and assembled the truth. The tea was light and sweet, slightly fruity in flavor, a nice change from the heavily spiced black tea Ahna was used to from home and she soon went back for a second cup.

While she wasn't able to come up with any good solutions to her current set of problems, she was at least feeling much more relaxed. There was nothing more she could do about her family's estate at that moment. Even should she forego her education and return home, any decisions she would make would likely only lead to additional confusion and frustration on the part of the land-holders. The tea was making her much sleepier than she had expected, so she decided to turn in early. Perhaps a good night's rest would help.

She woke to the scent of smoke and an eerie glow flickering across the room. Confused and drowsy, she pushed herself up in her bed, trying to determine what was causing the light. Orange figures danced through her vision, pirouetting in and out in the room's unnatural glow. She blinked in bewilderment, rubbing the swiftly-accumulating moisture from her vision. In stark contrast to the tears, sand seemed to fill all of the most sensitive spots in her eyes, refusing to be washed away. As the fog cleared from her mind, she realized that the glow, the figures, and the scent were all con-nected. Additionally, she could hear the crackling as the fire burned menacingly toward her through the small room.

Flames licked up the walls and crept across the

floor, engulfing everything in their path. Stone walls and floors blackened, soon appearing the same color as the heavy smoke that dripped from the ceiling. A thin haze of the miasma filled the lower areas of the room, not yet dense enough to block vision but more than enough to identify.

Choking on the smoke, which was much thicker and denser in her sleeping chamber than she had initially realized, she relied on her sense of touch more than sight to make her way to the door. She shied away from the strongest of the heat sources, hoping to not get burned during her escape, all memories of her protective sigils forgotten in the early morning panic. Despite the light, which grew brighter with every step, the smoke was too thick for her to be able to see much of anything at all, and when she opened her eyes, it burned. She could feel tears of pain dripping down her face as she called for help, her voice raspy and barely audible as she choked on the fumes.

Beyond her sleeping chamber, the smoke was thicker and the fire raged hotter. She could feel her skin drying out and soot covering her as she dropped to the floor, lungs on fire and unable to breathe. Confused, she tried to see the fire suppression sigils that had only just been placed along the halls, wondering how the flames could have grown so large with them in place. She was unable to locate any of the sigils because of the thick black miasma that continued to fill the area, burning her eyes more than she ever would have believed possible. Even the steady flow of tears was not enough to defend against the smoke. Coughing and sputtering, she covered her mouth with the edge of her sleeping clothes, hoping that would filter out the worst of the toxic fumes.

Crawling slowly and carefully, she moved across the floor, trying to stay as low as possible. Finally, she reached the exit at the end of the hall, hopeful that beyond the door would be breathable air once more. As soon as she wrapped her fingers around the handle, however, she jerked backwards in pain, her palm burned by the short contact with the heated metal. Choking back a cry of pain, she braced herself for the pain she knew was about to come, grasped the handle, and twisted.

The handle refused to turn.

"No!" she called out in despair. The utterance was involuntary and she immediately regretted it as her throat and lungs protested in response. She had long since run out of air.

Something glinted to her left and, without quite realizing what she was doing, she turned towards it. Her hand encountered what she first believed to be a wall but she soon recognized the shapely texture of a windowsill. Above the windowsill, her fingertips found the lowermost pane of glass, blessedly cold against the searing heat of the fire that surrounded her. She pressed against the surface but it remained intact.

Desperate, she angled herself against the window and, using her left elbow, hit the glass with what little strength the fire had not yet stolen. Relief flooded through her body, weakening her knees as she heard the glass shatter, pieces falling like millions of shooting stars to the ground far below. Smoke rushed out through the opening and Ahna was able to take the first breath of clear air since she had woken.

The danger was not yet over. While she was able to breathe somewhat better, she was still trapped. The window offered little hope for her desperate situation. While the opening offered precious clean air, releasing much of the noxious smoke in the process, it offered nothing by way of escape as the ground was hundreds of stories below. The roaring fire drowned out her own calls for help.

Without warning, she felt herself being lifted off of her feet. She shrieked as the ground fell away beneath her, wondering what fresh torture was about to be inflicted. Weightless, she floated through the open window and into the bracingly cold air outside. The sudden shift in temperature made the autumn air feel like icicles burrowing into her skin but she didn't care. Icicles were a welcome relief to her burned flesh. For the briefest moment, she wondered if she was being propelled to safety by one of her as-yet-unidentified sigil tattoos but then she discovered that she was being guided towards a man in the robes of a Magi.

Two students flanking him, Magi Tanis guided her safely to land on the walkway closest to her chambers. He and the nearby students obviously had been hard at work getting more of the trapped students to safety, if the four other people, each of whom was equally as disheveled as Ahna herself was, were any indication. As she sat upon the cold stone, coughing and choking out the last of the smoke, she watched as two more students were guided to safety by the Magi's expert hands.

"Well done breaking the window," Ahna turned to the speaker, one of the assisting students wearing a sixth-year sash. "If you hadn't, we never would have realized there was anyone in that hall." She was tall and lean, with wavy blonde hair that blew across her face in the wind but she didn't bother to move it, focused instead on the more important task at hand.

The other rescuer Ahna recognized as Phalant, one of the other students in Magi Tanis's class. He was turned away so that Ahna could only see him in profile but she recognized him immediately. Not for the first time, Ahna wondered how one person could be so good at so many things.

She waited on the safety of the walkway, huddled with the ever-growing group of evacuees, for almost half an hour until Magi Tanis and his assistants were satisfied that nobody else was trapped in the burning tower. Other Magi and students, some that Ahna recognized but many more that she didn't, ran back and forth, either on the ground or in the air, extinguishing the blaze. By the time the morning's first rays began cresting over the horizon, all of the flames had been extinguished. Those who had been rescued, Ahna included, were ushered into the unburnt tower.

Although it was obvious that the Academy staff was not expecting such a conflagration, they were at least prepared for the possibility. Within half an hour, all of the students who had been housed in the fire-damaged area had been assigned new rooms and what belongings they possessed that had not been damaged in the blaze were delivered to their new quarters.

As the students were led to their new rooms, Magi Andress pulled Ahna aside. "Please come with me for a moment," he said quietly as he led her in a different direction from where other students were being guided. She hadn't seen the magus among the rescue and fire-fighting teams but the wear on his face and the deep circles under his eyes showed that he had been actively involved in the efforts. He led her to his office, securely locking the door behind her once they were both inside.

"How did you survive that?" he asked as he settled into a chair next to her.

"I... I don't understand," she stammered in

response. The question took her completely aback. How could she possibly explain how she was alive? Beyond that, his question startled her by its meaning. Was she somehow in trouble for having survived the night? That couldn't possibly be right.

"I've just come from your room," he explained. "It's completely destroyed. It appears that the fire was set directly at your door, so the majority of the damage was within your chambers." He pulled his glasses from his face and, using the thumb and middle finger of the same hand that held his glasses, rubbed the bridge of his nose. "From what I can tell, your escape was virtually impossible."

"But the fire suppression sigils..." her voice trailed off as she recalled her inability to detect the sigils in the hallway and the thickness of the smoke she had managed to maneuver through. The sigils had only just been installed, they couldn't have just failed, could they? Perhaps one had failed, she could understand that. Even two wouldn't be outside the realms of comprehension. But there were simply so many of them so that it was virtually impossible for them to have all failed at the same time. That was precisely the reason why so many had been used to begin with.

"The official story of the fire is that it was caused by an accidental spellcasting by a novice student, probably a first- or second-year. That means there won't likely be much attention drawn to the fire beyond that."

"Accidental fire? How could all that have been caused by an accidental fire?" Ahna had seen plenty of damage from unskillful spellcasting but none of them had come anywhere near the devastation caused by the fire. "And how could an accident cause the fire wards to fail?"

Magi Andress held up a hand to calm her. "As I said," he answered calmly, "that is the official story. There are only a handful of people who know otherwise and we'd like to keep it that way." He placed the glasses back into their customary position before continuing. "Not only do we believe that this was an attack, we have plenty of evidence that it was targeting you specifically."

She sat back in her seat, stunned. Even though she had spent countless hours wondering whether the assassination of her father would continue on to an attack against her as well, it had always been just an idea. She had never really believed that she would be targeted, that she would be almost killed.

Her father was important, she herself was nobody to be feared. "Do you know who was responsible?"

"Not yet. The investigation is ongoing. We hope to uncover more in the morning, once we can get a better idea of precisely what happened.

"Furthermore, we have decided that, for both your safety and the safety of those around you, you will no longer be housed with the other students."

"I'm being evicted?" The idea of being forced to leave the school grounds horrified her. "Am I to be sent back home?"

"No, nothing as severe as that. We simply believe that the risk of damage is too great for you to live in an open area such as the dormitory hall. We are making arrangements to have you relocated to more secure quarters, where we can be certain no further attempts on your life can be made."

To her relief, nobody had died as a result from the fire but that was not a risk the Academy was willing to continue making. She silently followed the Magi as he led her to her new rooms.

6

"More secure quarters," Ahna grumbled to herself. "Feels more like a prison cell than a student's quarters."

The rooms she had been given were positively claustrophobic, less than half the size of the rooms that she had inhabited before the fire. She paced back and forth across her bedchamber, counting the steps with each pass. "One, two, three, four, five, six." Reaching the opposite wall, she turned back the opposite direction. "One, two, three, four, five, six." Her seating room, just past the bedchamber, was not much larger, only two paces larger across and three additional paces wide. Normally Ahna paced the larger room but she had quickly grown bored of that and moved to the smaller room for a change of scenery. "One, two, three, four, five, six."

For the last two weeks, she had been cloistered in these same two rooms, seeing only the bare walls on any given day. There were no windows to see outside and she hadn't been allowed to leave since being brought there the night of the fire. She didn't even attend her classes anymore; now the instructors came to her rooms to teach her individually. Her sitting room was littered with notes and books, remnants of those instructions and her own personal boredom. It wasn't entirely surprising that none of her friends had come to visit her. Ahna seriously doubted whether any of them knew where she was, let alone in what kind of situation she currently found herself.

More than anything, Ahna regretted not accepting Zavala's most recent outing invitation. Had she realized how soon she would be locked in this prison, Ahna would have taken her friend up on the offer of an afternoon adventure at the mysterious Dragon Keep. She stopped pacing in her bedroom and moved out to the sitting room, dropping into one of the stuffed armchairs that waited there. Between the two chairs sat a small round wooden table, which was currently covered with books and pages full of notes.

Thinking of Zavala led Ahna to wonder if her friend had put together the pieces of what had become of her. Although Ahna hadn't admitted to being a de Melville when Zavala had initially questioned her on the topic, there had been enough overheard conversations that could have easily led Zavvie to put the clues together. Additionally, she wondered if Zavala was suspicious of the fire. Ahna was still only beginning to develop her own personal theories as to the origin of the fire and how deeply enmeshed it was in the events of her own family. If Zavvie accepted that Ahna was the assassinated Count's daughter, it stood to reason that she would expect Ahna to be targeted as well.

"They can't really mean to keep me here forever, can they?" The question was rhetorical, as there was nobody available to answer. It would be another two hours before the next magus would arrive, two hours of loneliness and boredom in the rooms that were feeling smaller and more cramped by the day. She missed walking along the sky bridges, particularly the one at which she normally took her meals. She missed visiting with her friends and seeing the other students in her classes. Most of all, she missed sitting with Zavala as she chattered on about all of her ideas on everything.

The only reason she knew which day it was, along with how many days had passed, was because of the rotating visits from her instructors. Every day, a different topic was covered and she learned an entire week's worth of each subject in the two hours or so of individualized learning. Not that she needed the full amount of time, of course. She had always been relatively quick to pick up on the topics and spent much of her free time learning more about the theories and practical applications. It was because of this habit that when it came time to demonstrate her skills and knowledge, she was always in the top ranks. Staying among the top students was important to her, partly due to her own personal need for information and to ensure her family had no reason to remove her from the Academy for lackluster grades. Lately, however, she had found herself dawdling a bit on her studies, not because of loss of interest in the subject matter but more to encourage her instructors to stay just that little bit longer. They were the only other people she saw on any given day, her only reprieve from lonely solitude.

One benefit to her isolation was that she had free reign of the library's resources. In order to stave off boredom completely, she had begun requesting books on all sorts of topics from her visiting instructors, from sigils to mental arts to every other topic she could imagine. Careful to spread the topics across multiple Magi, Ahna was concerned on what would happen should anyone uncover what she was actually researching. Under normal circumstances, students were not allowed to remove more than a couple books and other materials at a time without express permission granted for each item, with a good reason provided for why the material needed to be removed from the library. Such permissions were rarely granted, so until now her research had been constrained by the library walls.

Given her current situation, along with how much of her free time Ahna was known to spend in the library, she had been granted special access to the library materials. Up to ten items at any given time could be entrusted to her care and she had been making good use of that access. She still hadn't managed to uncover anything about the Grand Coven but she had learned a lot more about sigils than she had ever expected to need.

Her research into sigils had initially started with curiosity about the markings on her own body and what each of the glyphs offered but her focus had shifted drastically the night of the fire. "Each one of these," she mumbled as she read through her notes, "should have been able to neutralize a fire about a quarter that size." As far as she could tell, with only a few of the suppression sigils activating, there should have been no fire damage whatsoever. "It wouldn't have taken more than three, perhaps four, to stop that size of fire completely. So why were none of them activated?" The fire certainly hadn't been so large when it had begun, it had grown substantially after having been set. From the very beginning, the sigils should have activated to halt the spread.

Any investigation that had been done by the Magi into that very matter was completely shielded from her. It seemed as though the Academy administration was satisfied that no students were actually killed in the fire, despite the numerous injuries she had herself seen, so they were happy to let their cover story of an accident stand. She dropped the stack of papers and picked up another one. "There are only so many reasons for sigils to fail. First, of course, would be that the sigils were improperly placed to begin with." She flipped through the pages. "Overpowering the sigils is another option," she sighed and flopped back in the chair. "That doesn't make any sense either. Someone would need to have an exceptionally high power level in order to do that."

While most of the students may have been willing to accept the official explanation, Ahna knew better. Even if she hadn't been explicitly told that the story was a lie, it wouldn't have taken her long to figure out otherwise on her own. "Sigils like that are actually quite powerful," she muttered as she jotted down more notes. "Basic fire resistance sigils are not that difficult but anything that is going to be attached to the walls of a place like the Academy is going to be well above the level of a first- or second-year student." On one of the pages, she had sketched a likeness of one of the marks, drawn from memory. "These are ornate, with lots of buried levels in them. I doubt even a sixth-year student came up with these."

There was one mark on the sigil that had frustrated Ahna since she began examining them. At first, she had thought that the squiggly little line had been a mistake, an error in her own memory, but the more she considered it, the less she believed that. "I think this may have to do with magical fires," she decided. Most fire-based sigils didn't bother to worry about the differences between magical and mundane fire, primarily because even a magically started fire turned immediately into a mundane fire as soon as flammable materials were ignited. Superficially, it made sense to include protection against magical fires into the sigils. As the halls of the tower were all made of stone, there would likely be a period of time between the ignition of a magical fire and the change to a mundane fire. However, that didn't feel quite right in Ahna's mind.

In her experience, if it didn't feel right, it was probably not quite correct.

"Okay, let's back up a step. What do we know? What are the facts involved? Let's not get buried in rumor, details, and should-haves." That was how her father had always guided her to rethinking a sticky situation. It had worked for her plenty of times before, so there was no reason to believe that it wouldn't work now.

"Fire suppression sigils are designed to activate as soon as they detect fire." That was the part that had been needling into the back of Ahna's mind. Warding sigils such as those along the hallway didn't require activation, the activation was built into them while they were created. That left only two options, neither of them comfortable. "Either someone really powerful disabled that portion of the sigils," she realized, "or those weren't actually fire suppression sigils at all."

Neither case was palatable. To modify an existing sigil required massive amounts of both skill and power, particularly when trying to modify multiple of them. Only a Magi was capable of doing that, as she seriously doubted that some unknown person had broken into the school to adjust the sigils. On the other hand, if the Magi had authorized the installation of sigils that were not suppression sigils at all, that led to even bigger problems. She could only believe that the small squiggle that she had identified in the mark had actually been the change from the original, functional sigil to the modified and non-functional ones that had been present in the fire.

"Magical fire," she arrived at the most likely conclusion. "These sigils don't protect against fire, they start them."

She sat back and looked at the drawing of the sigil in horror. Never before had a tiny curved line appeared so sinister. She reflected back on how many people other than herself had been rescued from the fire. "They could have been killed," she whispered.

She didn't want to admit, even to an empty room, that she had been the target. From what she knew about the other students who had been impacted by the fire, none of them were likely to be targeted for assassination. Although she had to remember that she herself was not known to be someone targeted by assassination attempts either, the likelihood of multiple people with circumstances similar to hers was far too small to consider at any great length.

Regardless of whether someone broke into the Academy to manipulate the sigils, whether they were deliberately tampered with by the Magi or whether they had been designed to be faulty from the start, there was one irrefutable fact: someone was going to great lengths to kill Ahna. The amount of planning and stealth indicated that whoever was targeting her wouldn't stop until they were certain she was dead. As she looked around her barren space, she strongly doubted that the prison cell she currently called home would be of much assistance if the assassin discovered where she was being held.

"No, it's worse than that," she corrected herself. "I am absolutely trapped in here. If someone were to come for me right now, I'd be completely defenseless."

She felt a bit silly for planning an escape from a building where she had intentionally refused to leave for the last few years, a building where until the fire, she had felt perfectly safe. Given the latest set of events, however, if whoever was targeting her learned of their failure, there was likely to be much more bloodshed and many more people hurt in the next attempt. "If someone is willing to set fire to the Academy to kill me," she reasoned, "they're not likely to just accept failure and move on."

The walls felt as though they were closing in

even tighter around her. Her mouth went dry and her temples throbbed as she considered what she was about to do. There was no reassuring window from which she could escape, not that it had ever been a good option. Flight, levitation, and most of the other transportation magics were simply not her strength and she didn't feel confident enough in her skills to risk it unless it was absolutely necessary. "If only Zavvie was here," she crossed her arms over the pile of papers and dropped her head onto them. "She's strong enough to catch me if I was to fall."

"What am I thinking?" She sat upright again. "Even if she was here, there wouldn't be anything she could do. It's probably better that she isn't here, after all. If she was near, she'd just be in danger as well. I need to do this on my own." She stared at the door that led beyond her rooms, the only exit from her cloistered existence.

She would have to time her escape just right. Luckily, she was reasonably certain that none of the Magi knew she was suspicious, so they weren't watching for her to make an escape. Her best chance would be while one of the instructors was coming to teach her the week's lesson, or while the instructor was leaving. So far, those had been the only times she saw the door open.

7

Ahna wasn't sure whether to be pleased or offended that the Academy staff didn't seem to be prepared for her to mount an escape. She had expected an amount of resistance as she crept through the stone hallways but so far there was none to be found. As she moved slowly and carefully toward freedom, she wondered if the ease of escape was by accident or design. When Magi Andress had taken her to her new residential quarters, he had been very clear that she was being kept there for her own safety, with plenty of words of reassurance that she would be guarded against all forms of attack as long as she remained where she was.

Just another thing that made Ahna suspicious. "So where are all of these safeguards you promised me?" she wondered, not for the first time. "Where are the elemental protection wards? Where are the alarm sigils? Where are the guards? Where are the locked doors?" Even the door that led out of her room had been left unlocked, a new twist that she wasn't sure how to interpret. Had her escape been somehow expected? Was it engineered, with plans set in motion with all the pieces in place for her to follow? Was she, instead of walking away from a trap, walking into one?

The last magus who had been in her room for a lesson had been Magi Tanis and she wondered if the mental arts instructor had somehow known about her plans. Even worse, she wondered if he had placed the idea into her mind himself. Although it felt like she was leaving the Academy of her own volition, was it really her decision to do so? Since mental magic had been her focus, her primary area of study for the last two years, she knew that memory manipulation was much easier than it appeared. So long as the correct sequence of actions to protect both the magus and the subject were understood and followed, it was perfectly safe and almost undetectable. The necessary sequence of steps was one that Magi Tanis knew as well; he had been the one to teach it to Ahna in the first place.

Memories could be erased, that was one of the easiest things to do, but more skilled magic users could modify memories to make the subject believe and remember things differently than how the actual events had transpired. In extreme cases, new memories could be completely fabricated so that the subject's entire history could be erased and replaced with the full knowledge of a new identity. Without the basic understanding of how mental magic worked, it was possible to completely erase the identity of a person and replace it with a fully-realized history, one that had never happened in truth. Memories of family and events that had never existed could be generated and placed, even memories of crimes committed in order to frame the innocent. Ahna had spent months reading book after book of similar horrifying stories of people who had used the mental arts in such nefarious ways. In fact, it had been to defeat just that type of activity in her own empire that had propelled her into that area of specialization to begin with.

As she approached the final portcullis, with the unsuspecting town of Three Rivers just beyond, she brought herself back into focus. She needed to stop worrying about whether she was acting in accordance with her own intentions or the intentions of someone else. "Okay," she said quietly. "What do I know? Stop wondering and take a look at the facts." Regardless of the origin of her current situation, she needed to pay attention to what she was doing. She had no real reason to believe that she was being manipulated, so her best plan was to stay the course. Even if she *was* being manipulated, the fact remained that she was in danger by staying at the Academy. The Magi had believed her to be safe in her rooms, which had subsequently been set afire. They further believed her to be safe in the unlocked and unguarded rooms from which she had just escaped. She no longer had any faith that the Magi could ensure her security, which was further confirmation of her reasons for having left in the first place. "You know what you need to do," she explained, imitating her father's stern voice. "Go on and do it already."

For the first time since arriving at the Academy three years previously, Ahna stepped out into the wider world.

Beyond the Academy walls was Three Rivers,

which she had briefly glanced at on her trip from the portal in Hub to the Academy. Given everything that had been happening during the time of her enrollment, there hadn't been much time for sightseeing or other exploration and she had not made up for that lack during her residency as a student. Now she found herself in an unfamiliar environment and unsure as to how to proceed. If she was being honest with herself, she never really expected her escape to succeed, so she had made very little plans for what to do once she was free. "Should have gone out with Zavvie more often," she mused to herself. "At least that way, I'd have a better idea of where to begin."

As she walked through the town, she spotted a tavern. "Might as well start there." At the very least, taverns were a good place to find out more about the area. From where she stood in Three Rivers, she wasn't even sure how to make her way to Hub. In her excitement to join the students at the Academy, she hadn't been involved in any of the travel plans and preparations on the journey into the Inland Empire. Her mother and father, along with a host of valets and other servants, had taken care of all the details. There had been no need for Ahna to worry at all about where she was and what was necessary in order to travel from one place to another. Her father and his assortment of valets no longer available, she needed to learn the ropes, and she needed to learn them quickly.

Inside the tavern, she ordered a meal and a glass of snowberry wine, unsure of what that was but curious to try it. Back home she had been accustomed to wine at suppertime but during her stay at the Academy no wine had been offered to the students. "Perhaps that's why Zavvie was always so eager to go into town," Ahna wondered. Not having expected any different, she was a little disappointed to not see Zavala's familiar face in the tavern. It would have been nice to have someone she knew nearby to guide her through her escape. That, and it had been weeks since she had seen her beloved friend and she missed her companionship dearly.

She quickly discovered that the townspeople of Three Rivers were only too happy to explain to her where she was in relation to other nearby towns.

"There's Wilee just a little bit to the north," one patron explained. He looked like a cleric, if his grey robes were any indication, but the massive warhammer at his side led her to doubt her initial assumption. While Ahna had heard of deities of battle and war, she wasn't exactly a follower of any of them so she didn't really know how to recognize any when she saw them. Despite her curiosity, she was reasonably sure it would be considered rude to ask, so she put the questions aside. She had more pressing matters to attend to, anyway.

"You don't want to go there, though," another was quick to add. "Wilee's surrounded by a forest that's infested with stillock spiders." This man appeared to be a northman, if his hide boots and breeches were any indication. He was well over six feet tall, as far as Ahna could tell from his sitting height, and it appeared that his light brown hair had never met the business end of a razor.

"Stillock spiders?" She hadn't heard of those before.

"Great big ugly mean things," the northman explained. "Nasty poison to 'em. You can tell where they are because there's thick white webbing all over the place."

Not excited about encountering spiders, ugly and mean or otherwise, Ahna decided that Wilee wasn't the direction to go. "What else is around here?" Ideally, she wanted to get back to the Dracott Empire so she could begin making her way home to Ruschlack but suspicion had started to take root in the back of her mind. If the assassin who had murdered her family, or the person who had paid for it to be done, suspected she was still alive, her life would likely be at risk upon her return. She needed to find out for sure who was responsible and she needed to figure out a way to return safely before staring the journey back to her homeland. In order to do that, she needed somewhere safe to start, somewhere away from Three Rivers. Somewhere nobody would think to look for her.

Preferably somewhere without big, ugly, mean spiders.

The cleric who had initially suggested Wilee looked thoughtful for a moment before answering. "There's a little village a little south of here called Hoem. I hear it's pretty decent."

"Isn't that where that trading company is headquartered?"

"Yeah," he agreed. "One of the McClannahans owns it, is what I hear."

The second man chuckled into his mead. "Durned McClannahans are everywhere, 's what I hear."

"Especially Hoem," the first agreed. "Even the mayor's a McClannahan there."

Curious as she was about the apparent prevalence of the McClannahan family, Hoem didn't sound like a big enough place to hide out in for any length of time. If there was nothing of sufficient size nearby in which she could hide, she would have to use the portal after all in order to make her way to another large town. "What about Hub?" she asked. "Isn't that somewhere around here?"

"Oh yeah," both of the men agreed simultaneously. "About a day by water is all."

That sounded about right for the amount of time she had spent on the trip from Hub to Three Rivers, so it sounded like the best option she had available. Since there was a portal in Hub, she would be more likely to get information about the Count and his family there than in Three Rivers, plus being a full day's travel away from any would-be assailants who may be watching for her in the Academy sounded like a great idea.

If she wanted to, she realized, she could even

make her way back home and find out what had really happened to her family. Despite her misgivings, familiar ground was always the easiest to navigate. Perhaps her initial hesitation was just a relic of her own childish fears. If that was the case, she would need to face them headlong and make a real, solid plan in order to succeed. If an assassin had traveled from the Dracott Empire to the Inland Sea to kill her, presumably the same assassin who had killed her family, he wasn't likely to turn around and head immediately back to the Dracott Empire in anticipation of her return. Maybe heading home was the best option after all. "All I need to do, then," she said quietly, "is find a boat to take me there." She looked back up at the men. "Can you tell me where I might find the docks?"

"Planning on heading that way?" the northman inquired.

Ahna nodded, unsure as to whether announcing her direction was a wise choice but she had no reason to suspect that these men, who she had randomly encountered in the tavern, could possibly be connected to either the Academy or the unknown assassin. Again, she wondered if there was some mental arts trickery afoot, but she saw nothing that made her suspicious. None of her protective sigils would guard her against such an intrusion and she wondered whether she could commission someone back home to add to her pattern. The feeling of distrust within her own mind was uncomfortable and the more she could do to safeguard against that concern, the better. Even if the sigil only offered minimal protection, that would be better than nothing.

"We're headed that way too," the cleric supplied. "Be happy to travel with you at least that far." He finished his drink and looked around the tavern. "From what I see, you're traveling on your own. That's not always the safest way to go, particularly for a lady like yourself. Least we can do is make sure you get there safely."

Hopeful that she wasn't making a poor decision in trusting the men, she agreed. "When would you like to go?"

"No time like the present," the northman answered for both men. "We're ready to go whenever you are."

8

Compared to the towns Ahna was used to back home in the Dracott Empire, Hub was a small town indeed. She and her two traveling companions, the cleric named Mikel and the northman named Vox, had boarded a ship bound for the island the previous morning, the day following their initial encounter in the tavern. Although the men had said it would take a day to reach the island from Three Rivers, it had actually taken just under two. The winds had not been favorable, the captain had explained apologetically to her when she had inquired about the delay. There was simply nothing he could do about it.

Ahna had briefly considered summoning some wind using what little elemental magic she had learned, but ultimately decided against it. If her absence had been discovered, which surely had happened by now, those searching for her would be looking for someone with magical ability, so the less she showed off her skills, the better off she would be. In the end it hadn't mattered after all, as the meager wind the sails managed to capture had been enough to guide them to their destination.

When she finally stepped foot on the docks of Hub, she looked up at the city for a long moment, evaluating where to go next and what needed to be done. She needed to find information, but other than traveling through the massive golden sphere that glinted with bright flashes of reflected sunlight as it slowly spun atop the city, there weren't any indications of where information could be found. Without better options available, she decided the tavern was the place to go. After all, she reasoned to herself, it had worked in Three Rivers. Before she did that, however, there were a couple other, more pressing, issues at hand that needed addressed.

The docks upon which she stood were barely higher than the water, evidence that tide was definitely high. Tier after tier rose before her, rings of town poised upon each tier as they rose higher and higher like a massive nuptial celebration cake, culminating in the golden sphere at the very top, the portal through which Ahna intended to continue her travels. At the end of the docks, a narrow street ran directly up the side of the hill, crossing each of the tiers in turn, offering quick access to all destinations. Young men with rickshaws parked nearby, calling for passengers to ride the hills instead of walking, a prospect Ahna found appealing.

"Here we are," Mikel explained with a one-armed gesture toward the town. "The very center of the Inland Sea." He lowered his arm and looked over at Ahna. "You sure you're going to be okay here on your own?"

"Yes," she answered, appreciative of his concern. "I will be fine, thank you." She clutched her cloak tighter against herself to guard against the brisk wind that blew in from the sea, whipping loose tendrils of her hair into her face. Almost as though in defiance of the journey they had just taken, the wind had finally picked up as they pulled in to the docks. She had long since given up on trying to brush the hair from her eyes, the wind simply sent more hair back in to replace it.

All of her concerns about the men with whom she had traveled across the sea had vanished along the journey, as neither of them had behaved in any manner other than honorable. A small part of her felt badly about her initial suspicion but she reminded herself that, in her position, suspicion could easily mean the difference between a long and happy life and a swift, violent death.

"Pretty girl like yourself," Vox added, "might draw a bit more trouble than you expected."

"True," Mikel nodded. "Promise me that if you end up needing any help, you'll come find us, all right?"

She agreed and watched as the unlikely pair headed off to explore the taverns. While accepting their offer to join them at the tavern sounded appealing and she intended to make her way to the tavern soon enough, she had other matters to attend to first.

During the short travel from Three Rivers to Hub, one of the other passengers aboard had inquired about her hair combs. The combs, given to her by her mother before leaving home, were family heirlooms, passed down from mother to daughter for more generations than she could fathom. She hadn't given a second thought to wearing the combs but the passenger's idle and seemingly-innocuous questions had made her realize that the combs were a form of identification, should someone be searching for her. Back home, at least, the combs would immediately identify her as a member of the de Melville family. While they were less recognizable this far away from her homeland, the risk was simply too great to ignore. This was particularly true in a town such as Hub, a town with a portal that could bring people from anywhere, even from the Dracott Empire, face to face with her. If any of the travelers nearby spotted the combs and recognized their significance, she could be in real trouble. Life outside the Academy was more fraught with danger than she had initially realized and there were still many things yet to learn.

She headed into town in search of the shopping district. Rickshaw drivers called to her as she passed but she paid them no mind. As appealing as they seemed, the funds in her pocket were all she would have until reaching home once more. Until that time, she couldn't spend her precious coin on fripperies. Walking up the hills quickly proved to be exactly as painful as she had expected but it was free. Thankfully, her years spent at the Academy, traveling up and down flights of endless stairs, had conditioned her muscles somewhat, else the trek would have been miserable indeed.

An hour and three shops later, she discovered a store that carried an assortment of magical items. While some of the items displayed prominently in the window to catch the attention of passers-by were priced much higher than they were worth, there were a handful of things that caught her attention.

"Can I help you find anything, miss?" the shop-keeper asked as she entered the store.

Ahna knew how she appeared. Her golden jewelry and fine slippers were a waving banner to indicate that she was a lady of means and she was used to the responses she got. Be that as it may, she had no intention of being swindled. Two of the first things she had been taught at the Academy had been how to identify magical items and how to determine the magical effects of an enchant-ment, both of which were skills at which she ex-celled. She needed no shopkeeper to tell her what she was looking at. Nor did she need someone to tell her the value of any magical item, at least not ones as common as the ones in the shop. Had the shopkeeper carried anything rare, she may have been out of her comfort zone but all of the items she saw were common enough.

A good portion of the items available in the store were training enchantments, pieces created by students. She spotted hot cups enchanted to keep liquids at a steady temperature, frost cubes imbued with elemental ice, and various other trinkets and knickknacks designed to make everyday life just a little bit easier. After only a few minutes of perusal, she finally found what she sought. "How much for the purse?"

From the outside, the purse in her hands appeared to be nothing more special than an ordinary, if high quality, bag. The enchantment placed upon it allowed it to carry a much larger volume than its external size would otherwise indicate, perfect for storing her valuables. The enchantment upon it was similar to that which she suspected had been placed upon the restricted area of the Academy library. Because of that, there was more than enough room within the purse for her to store her heirloom hair combs along with any other items she picked up in town. Although she knew she needed to remove her identifiable jewelry, she had no intention of leaving any of it unguarded and a small, inconspicuous bag that she could carry along with her was exactly what she was looking for.

On a nearby shelf, hidden behind a stack of cosmetics and creams, she spotted a grooming stick, a tiny wand that held an enchantment which changed hair color and style. She had used this type of wand before, her mother had one to arrange her hair in the ornate styles demanded by some of the formal affairs she attended. As a child, Ahna had loved having her mother sweep her hair into grand styles for nothing more exciting than an afternoon of board games and tea with finger sandwiches.

From the magic shop, she continued to explore the town. In an attempt to further blend in, she purchased some rough clothing from a different merchant. The clothes were nowhere near the fine silks to which she was accustomed but more akin to the clothing worn by the locals. They would allow her to blend in more effectively than the garments in which she had arrived in town.

Ahna loved her hair. She spent hours brushing it until it shone like the morning sunrise. Her mother had been particularly proud of Ahna's hair as well, constantly bringing her baubles and gems with which to adorn it. "I'm sorry, mother," she whispered to herself. "It's not permanent so I hope you'll one day forgive me." Much as she loved the color of her hair, she knew that it was another means of identifying her. Even among her own family, her hair color was rare. It was even more so this far from home.

After changing into the new clothing and storing her old wardrobe in the purse, she scanned the area to find someone with hair she wished to imitate. Spotting an attractive woman with lovely auburn hair, she deliberately bumped into her, touching her locks with the wand in order to absorb some of its color. Fifteen minutes later, Ahna's hair had been transformed into a brand-new auburn shade rather than the blond tresses to which she had been accustomed for her entire life. Examining her reflection in a store window, she would have been hard-pressed to see herself as a nobleman's daughter.

Looking like a commoner only minimized the

number of curious glances sent in her direction. Ahna wasn't stupid; she realized that she lacked a lot of the skills necessary to survive on her own for extended periods of time. She would need assistance if she was going to make it through this ordeal alive. Deciding that the risk of taking the cleric and the northman up on their offer was worthwhile, she turned back toward the dock area. "Now which tavern did they say they were heading for?"

It took scouring three different taverns before she finally located the men. Lound music poured out of the entrance, evidence that a traveling bard had located their new venue. Vox, ever the north-man, danced atop a table, albeit badly. His booted feet stomped almost in time to the music, rattling all of the mugs and plates on both the table upon which he danced and each table adjacent to it. His antics were entertaining, if the encouraging shouts from the other tavern patrons were anything to go by. Less inclined for attention than his friend, Mikel sat at a small table a short distance away, mug of ale in hand and a buttered crust of bread in the other, his warhammer resting comfortably next to him.

One glance at the pair of men was all Ahna needed in order to decide which of them to approach. She had no intention of interrupting the northman's fun and the last thing she needed was the amount of attention Vox was garnering. Most of the eyes in the tavern were riveted on the gyrating man. At the very least, she thought to herself as she wove through drunken revelers, all attention was on him and not on her. If she was to be spending much time in establishments such as this, she thought to herself, there may have been much less need for camouflage than she had expected.

Mikel smiled warmly as she approached and took a seat. Once she was settled and looked up to meet his eyes, his smile changed to an expression of surprise and his eyebrows retreated higher up his forehead. "Wow," he commented at last. "That's quite the change. I didn't recognize you."

"That's the point," she admitted. "My look earlier today was a bit too out of place. I figured a change of style was appropriate."

"Well, it worked," Mikel agreed. "You look completely different."

From the expression in his eyes, she could tell

that he wasn't completely believing her explanation but at least he had enough couth to hold his questions.

She signaled the barmaid for a glass of wine. "I thought about your offer," she said once it arrived. "I could really use a pair of guards to keep an eye on me until I get where I need to go." She took a sip of the wine, wishing it had been the same variety she had been able to get back in Three Rivers. Apparently, snowberry wine was a local specialty that was not readily available everywhere, to her disappointment. "I will pay both of you, of course."

Mikel nodded. "We've done our fair share of escorting people to and from. Where is it that you need us to bring you?"

"You see, that's the thing. I'm not sure where is a good place for me to be right now."

He raised an eyebrow yet again at that and took a swig of his ale. "Most people know where they are headed before hiring escorts, you know."

"I understand," she admitted, "but there are circumstances involved."

"What kind of circumstances?"

"The kind best not spoken of where ears can overhear."

He nodded his understanding and signaled to Vox, who dropped from the table with a heavy thud, solid enough to rattle the floorboards.

Ahna really wasn't sure how much information to offer the men. Asking for information about the Dracott Empire, particularly about her family, was likely to be dangerous. Asking about the Grand Coven, which by all accounts was nothing more than rumor this far east of her homeland, was likely to be equally dangerous, if not more so. She couldn't help but wonder if there was a connection between the assassination of her family and the Grand Coven, although she couldn't imagine what the connection could be. She had no doubt that the attack on her own life was connected in some way to the murder of her family. The coincidence was simply too great to believe otherwise.

"I wanted to come here to search for answers," she explained once Vox joined them at Mikel's table, fresh ale in hand. "This was a stop I made on my journey to Three Rivers so it made the most sense for me to come back this way as well." She took another sip of her wine and looked up to meet the men's eyes. "I'm at a bit of a loss as to what to do right now," she admitted. "This whole position is a little new for me."

"Maybe you should start by letting us know what you're looking for," Vox suggested. "Perhaps we'll be able to help you find it, whatever it is."

"I'm not sure you can." She lowered her eyes, willing the tears to remain hidden. "I'm trying to find out who had my family killed, optimally without getting myself killed in the process."

"Oh." Vox looked between Ahna and Mikel as though trying to assess the situation more clearly. "You need someone to watch your back so you don't get murdered."

"It's a little more than that. I don't need to find out who murdered my family, as I believe I already know that part. What I need is to know who hired the assassin responsible without letting them know who I am so that I don't become targeted as well."

"You know who the assassin is?" Mikel prompted. When she nodded, he asked, "who was it?"

Her voice dropped to barely louder than a whisper, far too quiet to be overheard in the bustling tavern. "It was the Dark Star."

"You're absolutely right," he said without missing a beat. When she looked up in surprise, he said, "about there being too many ears here. We should go somewhere quieter if we're to discuss this further."

Vox slammed his empty mug onto the table in agreement and heaved himself to his feet. "Then let's go," he said without preamble. "Lead the way."

"There are a few quiet places here in town," Mikel said, "but I'm not sure how comfortable you'll be there. Most of them will be pretty rough."

Ahna shook her head. Although she had gone to Hub with the intent of searching for answers, after some discussion with Vox and Mikel, who she wasn't yet completely certain she could fully trust with her secrets, she had only realized that asking around would bring her right back into the same danger she was trying to escape. "Instead of asking around here," she decided, "I think that Tradewinds would be a much better place to find answers."

"You sure about that?" Mikel asked. "Tradewinds is even bigger than Hub, so it's likely to have even more ears."

"Big is good, at least right now. More people

means that I can blend in a little better, it'll be less likely for me to be spotted in Tradewinds." There, she could find more distance between herself and Three Rivers but it was still not close enough to home for people to recognize her. Just because Tradewinds had a portal, she reassured herself, that didn't automatically mean that there were people there to search for her.

Once the men agreed to accompany her, much as they obviously didn't fully understand her motivations, she, Vox, and Mikel lined up to take the portal to Tradewinds. The line to take the trip stretched far away from the gleaming sphere, filled with dozens of people awaiting their turn through the gates. An assortment of vendors walked up and down the line of waiting passengers, offering snacks, beverages, and an assortment of trinkets for them while they waited. Ahna watched one particular vendor approach with interest, as she had skipped lunch and the pocket sandwiches he offered were tempting.

They were only waiting in the line for a matter of moments, not even enough time for Ahna to get the desired sandwich, before she heard someone calling her name. Certain that it had to be a mistake, someone calling to someone whose name simply sounded similar to her own, she risked a quick glance around.

Immediately she could identify that there was no name confusion. Standing no more than ten paces away, looking directly at her and waving to get her attention, stood Zavala.

9

"I heard you left the Academy," Zavala explained as she jogged over to join Ahna and her companions, ignoring the brisk wind that flowed across the tip of the island. She eyed the men critically as she did, apparently not expecting her friend to be traveling in such masculine company. "After everything that happened, I'm not surprised."

"How did you know where to find me?" Ahna couldn't suppress the sensation of joy that rose in her at the sight of her familiar face. The one person she had regretted leaving behind had managed to find her. Somehow, she wasn't altogether surprised.

Zavala shrugged noncommittally. "I went looking for you after the fire but you were nowhere to be found. When I realized you were gone, I figured you might have left to go home or something after that. It wasn't until I was in the library a few days ago and overheard one of the Magi asking about some books for you that I knew you were even still there." She stepped into the line, nudging Vox aside as she did. "Hey, excuse me there, buddy," she smiled at the large man who nodded affably in return and stepped aside to give her more room. "Took me a few days to figure out who would be the best to ask about where they had you hidden away. It wasn't until I cornered Magi Tanis this morning, demanding to see you, he told me that you disappeared last night.

She shifted her weight from foot to foot before continuing. "I have to admit, I wasn't altogether surprised that you left. After everything that happened, first with your family being assassinated and then with that awful fire in the dorms, I figured you were probably on your way home. If I was going to catch up with you, here's where I figured I'd have my best chance; Hub is the closest town with a portal, after all." She clutched her cloak tighter around herself to keep it from slapping against others who were waiting nearby.

When Zavala mentioned her family, Ahna

moved to shush her friend. "I don't want anyone else knowing about that," she reminded the older girl. To her relief, none of the others waiting in line appeared to have overheard. Or, if they had, they showed no reaction to Zavala's comment.

"Oh, don't worry," Zavala reassured her. "Here, nobody cares who you are. For all anyone will notice, you're just another traveler who chose the longest line in town to wait in. Love what you did with the hair, by the way. Great color."

"Thank you" Ahna responded automatically. "Does this mean that everyone at the Academy knows what's going on?" Although she had no intention of returning to the Academy, she was saddened to hear that her disappearance had been noticed. For as much time as she spent on her own and not interacting much with the other students, particularly over the last few weeks, she had hoped that her absence would be less notable. It appeared that was not to be the case.

"Nope," Zavala reassured her again. "Most people haven't really noticed anything unusual, other than the standard gossip and random conspiracies about the fire. You being gone after it was all said and done hasn't really been much of a conversation point.

"Furthermore, I agree with your decision to leave, I just wish you'd have let me know you were going. The Academy obviously isn't safe for you anymore. In fact," she stepped closer and leaned down to speak conspiratorially, "I'm starting to think maybe the whole legend about the Grand Coven and their presence in Three Rivers might be a little bit less of a myth than we had originally thought."

"But you said that was just a legend, rumors spread by upperclassmen to scare all of the new students," Ahna reminded her, her voice equally low and quiet. Although she knew more than most that the Coven was much more real than Zavala's previous dismissal, there was no reason for Ahna's suspicions to cause further troubles for her friend. On the other hand, she was curious to hear what, if anything, Zavala had uncovered in Ahna's absence.

"True, very true. But the more I think about it, the more I think that maybe there really is a group of them within the Academy, perhaps even within the ranks of the Magi themselves." With a scowl, she reached up to run a hand over the wildly-fluttering hair, tucking as much as she could behind each ear. The spell that had caused her hair to turn into vibrant blue feathers had continued to fade, as evidenced by the scant handful of feathers that remained among the tresses.

"Grand Coven?" Mikel interrupted. "Who are they?" He looked down at Ahna, his forehead creasing in concern. "Are you hiding from someone?"

"Nothing you need to worry about," Zavala raised a hand and held it between the pair of girls and the men, palm facing away as she answered on Ahna's behalf. "While I'm sure you boys are both perfectly capable, I think we'll be just fine without your assistance."

"No," Ahna stopped her, reaching out her own hand to lower Zavala's. "It's okay. I've hired these men to guard me until I get home." She quickly made the introductions, mentally kicking herself for having not done so sooner. Circumstances notwithstanding, her mother would be appalled at the lapse in manners.

"You hired them?" Zavala looked between the fur-clad man and the one carrying the massive warhammer, suspicion heavily weighting her gaze as she perused each in turn. "How do you know they can be trusted? They could have been sent by the same people who killed your family."

Vox looked surprised at her statement while normally stoic Mikel appeared thoroughly offended. "You... you really think that we..." the cleric sputtered. He took a half step backwards, as if to physically distance himself from the very idea.

"Not at all," Ahna reassured him, placing a hand on his arm. She could feel the muscles beneath his cloak, tensed and ready to defend both her and his own honor at the insult. Until Mikel's outburst, she had thought that the northman would be the more temperamental of the two. Men and women of the northern lands were known far and wide for their honesty and integrity, stories she had heard even in her own homeland. For Zavala to even suggest that he was anything less than such was an insult - not just to Vox but to his people as well. That reputation for integrity had been one of the driving forces in her decision to trust the men in the first place. She turned back to Zavala. "They didn't approach me, I approached them. There's no way they were sent to kill me."

"But they're strangers. How do you know they can be trusted?"

Ahna was fairly certain that the only reason Mikel wasn't speaking more was due to the restraining hand on his arm. She could understand Zavala's point, her own safety was a high concern for her as well. It was reasonable for Zavala to be anxious and worried about her. Be that as it may, she had a strong feeling that she could trust the men, despite her own suspicions and the short amount of time that she had known them. "Calm, Zavvie," she said gently. "I am safe here. There is nothing to fear."

"You don't understand," Zavala responded, her voice far more serious than Ahna had ever heard before. "You remember what I said about the Grand Coven being nothing more than a scary story, I know you do. You just mentioned it yourself. But that wasn't entirely the truth." She lowered her voice further so that it was barely above a whisper. Ahna had to lean in closely to be able to hear her as she continued to speak. "I know for an absolute fact that the Coven is more than just a myth." She traced a small circle in the dirt with the toe of her boot before continuing. "I've known the whole time. I just didn't want to scare everyone."

Ahna's eyes widened in surprise at her proclamation. "How do you know that?"

"Because my mother was a member." Zavala lowered her glance to her feet, shuffling her toes across the rough cobblestone pathway as she admitted the truth. "I didn't want anyone to know, it's so shameful."

It wasn't until she felt Mikel's other hand, large and warm, cover her own hand that Ahna realized how tightly she was clenching his forearm. "Perhaps we should discuss this elsewhere," he suggested gently. "Here is not the best place for conversing on such matters."

"You're right," Ahna agreed. She certainly wouldn't want to discuss her own family's most private issues in front of a crowd of people and there was no reason to have Zavala do it either.

"I know of a teahouse nearby. It should be relatively quiet at this time of day."

"A teahouse?" Ahna looked up at him in surprise.

"Absolutely. I make it a point to stop by there every time I'm in town."

"But…" Ahna was at a loss for words. Somehow, she couldn't imagine the pair of travel-worn men in a place as refined as a teahouse. Perhaps tea houses in Hub were different from those to which she had been accustomed back home. "I suppose that will work," she conceded finally. She just hoped that here, tea wasn't some sort of alternative term for something unsavory.

"What?" Mikel chuckled at her obvious confusion. "Just because I am a man, you assume that means I can't enjoy an occasional cup of tea?"

"No, of course I didn't mean it like that," Ahna was quick to respond, her cheeks warming as she realized the fallacy of the assumption to which she had just leapt. If she knew anything about her new companions, it was that they were honorable and respectable men. There had been nothing outside of her own ignorance to make her believe there was anything unsavory in his suggestion. If Mikel said that their destination was a tea house, she would believe him. She lifted her chin and straightened her back. "Let's see this tea house of yours."

They followed the cleric as he led them away from the portal and down into the thick of Hub's commercial district. It wasn't the same area of the commercial district where Ahna had previously been shopping, instead he led them through a quieter area of the town. There, the shops had potted foliage out front and small tables with overhead umbrellas dotted the pathways, colorful and shade-covered areas for patrons to rest and take in the amazing view of the Inland Sea. Each storefront looked more inviting than the last and Ahna hoped that at some point she would have the opportunity to return to Hub in order to explore them more closely.

They stopped in front of a shop, the opening of which was flanked by a pair of glass-topped tables with umbrellas the color of the sea for shade. A pair of elderly ladies were seated at one of the tables, each of whom was at least seventy years in age, who greeted Mikel as they approached.

"My boy," one of them called over to him, her voice belying the age written into her skin. "Back again, I see." She was dressed in a long, loose skirt with a cream-colored apron covering her front. The apron had powdery blue ruffles running around the bottom and sides with tiny pink and yellow flowers embroidered into it, the pattern of which was matched by the ruffled clip holding her milk-colored hair away from her face.

"Of course," he responded with a warm smile, "I can never stay away from your shop for very long. But I think that today, my friends and I would appreciate an amount of privacy."

The woman looked at the ragtag group but made no comment as to their appearance, nor did she question their need for privacy. "You may take the room in the back," she offered without hesitation. "And take as long as you need. I will have a pot sent in shortly."

Once the group was settled in the cozy back room of the tea shop, a powder blue ceramic pot of steaming hot tea was delivered along with an assortment of equally brightly-colored cups with matching saucers. They were quicky joined by a plate of sugar cubes with silvery tongs, a small pitcher of cream, and a bowl of lemon wedges. After the door to the back room was securely closed to ensure no further interruptions, all eyes turned to Zavala.

"It's true," she started. "I know I said that all of the rumors about the Grand Coven were just to scare the new students at the Academy but I never truly believed what I was saying. I discovered many years ago that my mother was a member of the Coven. In fact, that was one of the main reasons why I left home when I did." She swirled her cup of tea, refusing to meet anyone's eyes as she spoke. "I didn't want anyone to know about any of this," she said finally.

At Mikel's questioning look, Ahna explained about the Grand Coven and what their presence in the Inland Empire meant. "They absolutely destroyed Tomens, so I can hardly imagine how much damage they would do out here." She hadn't expected to discover that Zavala had such a close relationship to the Grand Coven as that to which she had just admitted and could easily understand why the girl had been uninterested in divulging that information to the other students. Now, knowing what she did, Ahna felt a bit more secure about Zavala's knowledge of her own personal family secret. With both of them in possession of information about the other that neither of them wanted released, it resulted in an amount of safety that neither of them would breach each other's trust in fear of their own secret being divulged.

"Sounds serious," Vox offered. "But what can we do to stop a bunch of powerful mages?"

"Not much," Mikel admitted. "I think Ahna's right. If they really are targeting her, regardless of their reasons for doing so, the best option she has to stay safe is to get as far away from here as possible." His glance moved from Ahna to Zavala. "No offense," he said, "but if you were able to find her here, it only stands to reason that others will be able to do so as well."

"Probably even more easily," Vox added. The teacup, already small in size, all but vanished in his enormous hands as he sipped daintily at the cup.

"That's why I need to get back home," Ahna explained. "It's about as far away from here as I can get."

"I'm not sure that's your best option, though," Zavala said. "You were headed for where, Tradewinds?" When Ahna agreed, she continued. "I think that's still a bit too obvious. While Tradewinds is a bigger town, sure, it's more than large enough to hide in for a little while but that kind of cover won't last for long. I think you need to be somewhere a little further away. Tradewinds is still a bit too close for comfort."

"And just as easy to trace where you've gone," Vox added. "If I was looking for you and I believed you had come here, that'd be the first place I looked next."

"Where would you suggest, then?" Ahna directed the question not just to Vox but to all three of her gathered friends.

Zavala thought for a moment before offering, "Sapphire."

Ahna blinked in surprise. "I hadn't considered going to Sapphire. I've never even been there."

"Think about it," Zavala said as she looked from Ahna to the two men. "It's a nice big town, bigger even than Tradewinds, and the Coven doesn't have much reach there. If you've never been, that makes it even less likely for someone to be looking for you there. Plus, it's far enough away from the Dracott Empire that your identity shouldn't be obvious, even if the enchantments you've got hiding your hair color should fail."

Her idea had merit, Ahna had to admit. "I suppose it could work," she said finally. "As long as I'm not discovered going through the portal, I should be safe enough there."

Vox thought it sounded like a great idea. "I

love Sapphire," he downed the last of his beverage. "Been too long since I've been there."

Mikel seemed less convinced. He pulled Ahna to the side as the group headed outside to make their way back to the portal. "Are you sure about this? Something just isn't feeling right here."

"I'll be fine," she smiled up at him, watching her friend dart through the air above. "Zavvie's been my best friend for three years now. I trust her more than I trust anyone, so if she thinks I'll be safer in Sapphire, I believe her.

"Besides," she added as they headed up the hill in the center of the town, "I've spent a lifetime hearing about Sapphire, so I'm excited to finally see it at last!"

10

Sapphire, the capital city of the Sapphire Empire, was one of the single most massive cities Ahna had ever seen, rivaling even the immense grandeur of Tomens. Although she had been unimpressed with most of the towns she had seen within the Inland Empire, Sapphire left her speechless.

The gleaming city perched upon a cliff that jutted out into the Azul Sea, which was easily six hundred feet below. Even the tallest waves in the most severe storms would be hard-pressed to reach the town above. On a clear day, such as the one when Ahna and her group arrived, the view was breathtaking as the clouds stretched lazily over the deep blue water.

The vast cityscape atop the peninsula was only

a small portion of Sapphire's splendor, as carved into the cliffside were more levels of the city, each of which opened to the amazing panorama of the sea. Massive stone pillars were placed at regular intervals throughout the lower levels, each supporting the levels above. It was an amazing feat of architecture that kept each level standing steady despite all appearances that the layers would crash down atop each other at the slightest provocation. Atop the cliff, stretching high into the sky, a sprawling metropolis bustled with people from all walks of life, many more than Ahna had seen in any one place in her life. Just about anything one could ask for was offered for sale, either by storefront sales counters or by sidewalk hawkers. Its tallest buildings were connected by a series of rope and wood bridges, suspended between the buildings to create multiple levels of pathways through the air. These clever routes served both as impressive architecture in their own right and a more serviceable purpose, easing the congestion on the tightly-packed streets below.

People by the thousands, far more than Ahna had seen in one place since the last time she had visited the capital city of Tomens, milled through the streets. Some went about their normal daily business of selling wares, others browsed the hundreds of storefronts. As they joined the throng, Ahna began to feel more at home than she had since leaving Ruschlack. Although the sights were definitely different than those in which she had spent her youth, the feelings that washed over her were the same. Pangs of homesickness joined the more comforting sensations as she realized that even if she did manage to make her way back home, home would never again be as she remembered it. Her mother wouldn't be at the family estate to greet her. Her father wouldn't be offering to take Ahna along on trips to Tomens when business matters demanded his attention.

"Where do you want to start?" Mikel asked, looking down at her in concern.

"I need to find out more about what happened to my family," she explained, pulling herself out of her reverie. "I know I said I wanted to go back home – and I still do - but until I know that it's safe for me to do so, there isn't much point." The last thing she wanted to do was to walk into an ambush of some sort. Without knowing what she was up against, that was precisely what would happen had she followed her initial instinct to blindly run home. Not for the first time, she was glad that her friends had dissuaded her from taking the portal in Hub directly to Tradewinds to go home.

"Makes sense," Vox nodded.

"I thought you knew what happened to them," Zavala pointed out. "Hadn't you been told while you were still at the Academy?"

"Not exactly," Ahna answered. "I was told that they were killed but I don't have any answers for why or by whom. If I go back now, that's likely going to be my fate as well before long."

"Didn't you say it was the Dark Star?" Vox asked.

"That was what I heard but it doesn't answer much. If he really was the one who ultimately did the act, that doesn't answer who hired him or for what ultimate purpose. People like that don't generally kill for their own gain, outside of the financial reasons." She considered explaining that she had doubts as to the notorious assassin's involvement in the first place but decided against mentioning it. There didn't seem to be much need for further confusion about an already tangled situation.

"What about that coven thing?" Vox asked. "D'you still think they're involved somehow? Could they have been the ones to hire him?"

"I really don't know," she admitted. "After learning what happened to my father, I spent a lot of time trying to determine what could have happened to the rest of my family, who would have had something to gain or would have some sort of a reason to hurt my parents. I didn't really look too deeply into investigating the Grand Coven, partly because I didn't see much of a correlation between my parents and that group and partly because the Academy didn't have any information about the Coven at all. As far as I could tell, there was no link between them and why this had been done. Everything I uncovered indicated that it was the Dark Star that killed my family, not the Grand Coven."

She blinked back the tears that threatened to surface before continuing. "It's still all so confusing and I barely even know where to start. I don't really have any good answers yet but I'm hopeful that someone here will have heard something more than what I have found."

"I doubt the Grand Coven has anything to do with that," Zavala said, her voice soft and soothing. "If you think about it, your father was probably killed for political position. Not only would the Coven not need to go that far for something like that, its even less likely that they would need to hire an assassin. After all, what would an assassin be able to do that a group of powerful witches couldn't?"

The sea belonging to the Sapphire Empire extended for miles away from the coastline but nowhere near the center of the Azul Sea. That expanse belonged to the Dracott Empire, the nearness of which had led Ahna to her conclusion that answers may be available in Sapphire. Not only because of its size and dense population but also because of its proximity to her home lands made it a valuable source of information. All of those factors indicated that information about occurrences in her hometown was more likely to be found there than in the Inland Empire.

"I'm not sure I really want to spend a lot of time asking about the Grand Coven here," she said. "I know that, at least at one point, they were really active in the Dracott Empire but I don't know whether they have any influence here in the Sapphire Empire or not and I don't think I am prepared in case they really are here." She looked around at her group of companions and added, "or rather, I don't think we are prepared." Most of them were likely more prepared to face anything than she alone was, that had been the very reason she currently traveled in a group instead of on her own.

"Do you really think they are that much of a threat to you?" Mikel looked even more concerned as he asked the question. "If so, then perhaps we should travel somewhere else, somewhere you will be safer." As though it was an unconscious movement, his hand lowered to trace the symbol of his deity, etched into the head of his warhammer.

"I don't think there really is much of a place I will be safer," Ahna laughed, "and if they really are here, there isn't a lot I would be able to do about it. What I can do," she turned to head down a side street that led to one of the suspended bridges, "is find out what I can about my family. That has to be my starting point."

She hadn't expected many people in the Sapphire Empire to have even heard of her family, let alone have any information as to their demise. At most, she had expected to find nothing more than the rumors she had already heard in Three Rivers, or perhaps exaggerations thereof. To her surprise, however, she discovered that the death of the Count de Melville was a topic of conversation almost everywhere they went. His assassination had become common knowledge, as was the belief that the assassin known as Dark Star was to blame. Somehow, she had expected for the gossip to have faded, at least a little bit, in the time between his death and her questioning, an unmet expectation that she was equal parts saddened and heartened to discover.

"Sounds like everyone here's heard of 'im," Vox said after hearing the report. "He's a pretty famous assassin."

"Me too," Ahna admitted. The Dark Star was the terror of the Dracott Empire. Stories abounded of the assassin's lethal exploits and his equally lethal hooked swords. Much as the idea terrified her that she was dealing with the efforts of a cold-blooded killer such as he, Ahna knew that she had finally found her starting point. Despite her initial hesitation to believe his involvement, it was sounding more and more that the information had been accurate after all. Now she just needed to uncover information on where to find him.

Given the nature of his particular business, she didn't expect that to be easy at all.

"Sounds like the bounty on him has increased," Mikel said as they left the offices of yet another local historian. While the bounty on the assassin had been high, it had been increased yet again, the funds coming from a surprising source. One of the guilds in Rex, a small town along the northern border of the Dracott Empire, had recently lost their guildmaster to the assassin's blades. In response to that death, the guild had added an additional hundred foutas to the price on the Dark Star's head, double if he was brought in alive.

Perhaps it was less about father, she mused, *and more the notoriety of the assassin that kept the whispers moving.* And notoriety was definitely the assassin's stock-in-trade, as she was hard-pressed to ask anyone about him without receiving at least some small tidbit of information. While most of the news she uncovered were rumors and legends that had begun to spread long before her own absence from society, other pieces of news were more recently developed. She just wondered how many of the stories she heard were true and how many were exaggerations. *Nobody can be that good, can they?* she wondered. *And if he truly is that prolific, how come he hasn't been caught yet?* Even beyond not being caught, nobody seemed to have even the faintest idea what the assassin looked like. "How can they catch him," she asked quietly, more to herself than to anyone else, "if they don't even know who they're looking for? He could be anybody, anywhere."

"Wonder why he went after a guildmaster," Zavala floated down to her friend after eavesdropping from the air above. "Don't people like that usually work for guilds?"

"Maybe he was hired by a competing guild," Ahna suggested. "It happens all the time with lawful organizations so I can't imagine it would be any less likely within unlawful ones."

"Good point," Vox agreed as they stopped at a street vendor to purchase some marinated chicken skewers. "My coin'd be on it being a lot more likely in places like that."

"I think I need to find him." Ahna didn't bother to look at her friends as she spoke, she could feel their surprised and disapproving looks without visual confirmation. "Not only would he know who hired him, he might even know the reasons for it." She fell silent for a moment before adding, "he may even tell me what the lives of my family were worth." How much coin, she wondered, had exchanged hands? What price did her father's blood fetch? Had the assassin been tasked to eliminate only her father, or were her mother and brother included in his charge? *Worse,* she thought, *was he tasked with eliminating the whole family?* By seeking him, was she seeking nothing more than her own death?

"I know this is important to you," Mikel said as they continued walking, "but are you sure this is the path you want to take? An assassin like that is dangerous. If you do manage to uncover his identity, no easy feat I'm sure, then he's more likely to kill you than to tell you who hired him."

"I know that," she whirled on him, her face far angrier than he had seen previously. Even

Zavala was taken aback by the response from her normally mild-mannered friend. "But it's the only chance I have. He's the only person who can tell me what happened to my family."

"We're just worried about you," Mikel said gently. "None of us wants to see anything happen to you."

"I'll be fine," she reassured him with false bravado. "If he wanted me dead, I would have been dead already. You have certainly heard the same things I have, possibly even more so. If he wanted me to be dead, if I was one of his assignments, then I wouldn't be here speaking with you right now."

Despite her assurances, Ahna knew that she was no match for anybody, let alone a trained killer. Even if she did manage to uncover the identity of the assassin, a feat that none who had attempted previously had succeeded in doing, she didn't know what to do with the information. Turning him into the guards was the most reasonable course of action and would result in his being punished for his crimes but it would offer her none of the answers she sought. She just hoped that, in the slight chance of her discovering who he was and, with an even smaller chance, being able to locate the man, she would figure out a way of convincing him to divulge the source.

Then, and only then, she would turn him over to the constables.

After a full day of investigating, with very few results, the group retired to an inn on the second level of the city, with a view overlooking the sea. The room was lovely, far more spacious than the tiny suite in which Ahna had been housed during her sequestration at the Academy and she opened the balcony doors to let in some of the fresh sea breeze. As the sun dropped below the horizon, spreading pink and violet waves of color across the sky, she sent a wish to the spirits of her parents. "Please help me," she requested. "Lend me your strength to get through this and to return home safely." A small flock of seabirds took flight at her words, which she chose to accept as a sign that her words had been accepted and brought to the heavens for her parents to hear.

Once the last glimmer of sun had disappeared from view, allowing the rising moon and stars to shine at their brightest, she sealed the doors once more, mindful of the presence of robbers and other thieves who would be present in a town the size of Sapphire. The last thing she needed was to lose what few possessions she still had while she slept. Moments after she landed on the pillow, exhaustion from the journey so far overtook her and she fell into a deep sleep.

She dreamt of the fire that had chased her from her rooms at the Academy. She could feel the heat from the fire as it stormed through the room, burning and immolating everything in its path, transforming everything she had known and loved into ash and ruin. She coughed on the remembered scent of smoke, which woke her from her slumber. Eyes stinging in the memory of the pain-filled night, she blinked around, willing her eyes to focus and wondering if she was still asleep after all. Smoke, transferred from her nightmares to the waking world, continued to fill her lungs and the roar of fire was even louder than it had been in her dream.

She blinked around in confusion, trying to understand how the fire from her dream had managed to manifest in her room. Spells existed to perform such a feat, of that she was certain, but none were spells that she knew. Even if she did know them, they required specific intent, intent which she lacked.

The doors that led further into the inn were still sealed but the balcony doors had been blown apart by the conflagration, all that remained attached were wooden fragments hanging limply on their hinges. The lamp that had rested on the small table next to her bed had broken from the heat, spilling oil that now ran in rivers of flame to the boards below. The bedcovers had caught as well, a trickling line of fire slowly crept upwards from the foot of her bed towards her unprotected face. Shrieking in terror as the reality struck her and she understood that this was no dream, she thrust the burning blankets away from herself and rolled, collapsing to the floor on the opposite side of the bed as the fire.

As she crawled, once again, through a burning room heading for safety, she noticed that her legs were in pain. Thinking she had trailed a foot through one of the numerous small fires that dotted the room, she glanced back to discover that the smoldering blankets had wrapped around her foot and her night clothes were on fire as well.

She kicked wildly, trying to dislodge the fire

from her body. The burning cloth stuck to her skin as though it had been glued there and refused to budge. Whimpering in equal parts pain and fear, she slapped at the embers, knocking burning bits away from her legs and onto the floor, finally managing to extinguish the fabric still adhered to her skin. No longer actively burning, she turned once more to head for the door. Vaguely, she could hear someone whimpering and crying. Just as vaguely, she recognized the sounds as coming from her.

Hopefully the hallway wouldn't be on fire, she thought to herself. Even more hopefully, the door wouldn't be locked.

Halfway to the door, it slammed open with a violent thud, ripping the sturdy lock from the jamb and impacting the wall behind it with enough force to break apart the painted plaster coating. Splinters of fractured wood and plaster rained down, adding more fuel to the fire and filling the air with fine particles of dust. Vox rushed into the room, jumped over the line of fire caused by the broken lantern, and plucked Ahna from the ground, cradling her gently and carefully in his massive arms. He turned and, after leaping back across the flaming river to the relative safety beyond, carried her toward the door.

"Wait," she called up to him, still coughing and choking on the smoke she had inhaled. "My bag. I need my bag." Without bothering to answer, he reached down and snagged the bag with two fingers of one hand as he passed.

He carried both her and her bag downstairs where a large crowd had gathered. All of the inn's guests had been evacuated by the innkeeper regardless of whether their rooms had caught fire yet. As a result of the activity, dozens of people milled about in the courtyard outside, safely away from the hazards inside. Most were gathered into small groups, discussing in hushed tones about the fire and exchanging theories about from where it had started, as well as scattered conversations about whether any of the inn's guests had been consumed by the flames. A robed form was hunched over a small child, wrapping a bandage around the boy's arm and reassuring him that he would be fine. "Just leave this bandage here for a few days," he explained to the frightened child's mother, "and it will be good as new."

"Found her," Vox said as he stopped in front

of the cleric. "Looks like she got burnt a bit." He turned to show Ahna's wounds to Mikel, careful to not touch any of her blackened skin.

"This looks pretty bad," Mikel breathed out through clenched teeth. His hair was unkempt and a shadow covered the lower half of his face, evidence that he had been woken by the fire as well. "Set her down on this bench here," he indicated a low stone bench nearby, "and I'll see what I can do."

Far more gently than Ahna would have expected from the northman, he placed her onto the bench where Mikel had indicated. Once she was settled, he stepped backwards to give the cleric enough room.

Mikel knelt on the ground in front of her and carefully nudged the burnt cloth aside, peeling it away from the skin so he could see her injury more clearly. Leaning in more closely to examine her, he furrowed his brows in confusion and then looked up at her. "This isn't nearly as bad as I thought it would be. It looks like you've barely taken any damage at all."

"Still hurts, though," she responded through gritted teeth of her own.

"I believe it. But I think that you just need a little salve and you'll be good as new." He reached into his own bag and pulled out a small jar of foul-smelling paste. As he spread the concoction over her legs, the pain subsided immediately. "With that much burning on your clothes, I had thought the damage would be much worse."

"I have some protection against fire," she explained once he was finished. "Sigils on my back. My whole family has them."

He nodded at the explanation. "That would explain the minimal damage. I still want to keep an eye on this burn of yours. Although it still doesn't look very bad, I want to ensure it doesn't get infected."

They spent the next couple hours in the courtyard, Ahna resting while Mikel treated other victims of the fire. Most people had managed to escape relatively unscathed but a few had required more substantial methods than just Mikel's burn salve. She watched with interest as he held his massive warhammer, which had been kept at his side the whole time, over one young woman who had been quite badly burned. As he closed his eyes and prayed, the hammer began to glow a pale green. As Ahna and all of the other onlookers watched, the man's injuries began to heal.

That was the first time Ahna had witnessed actual clerical magic in person. She had heard of it, certainly, but hadn't ever gotten the opportunity to witness it. While she had noticed the symbol of his deity engraved on the weapon, she would never have expected that the warhammer Mikel kept close by was actually his holy symbol, his dedication and connection to his deity, but it made a lot more sense now that she had seen it in action. If absolutely nothing else, the expression of pure rapture on Mikel's face as he communed with his deity to cast the healing magic was a sight to behold. Ahna had never seen anyone in such a state of contentment, of pure bliss, and she had to admit it made her slightly jealous.

Just once, she thought to herself, she would like to know what that felt like.

In the meantime, the fire brigade had been running into and out of the building, extinguishing the fires everywhere they were located and dampening cinders before they could blossom into full bloom. By the time that Mikel had finished tending to all of the wounded, the fires had been put out and the building was once again declared safe. Those whose rooms had remained untouched during the ordeal shuffled back inside, eager to return to their night's repose.

Ahna, along with a handful of others whose rooms had taken the brunt of the fire's damage, was given a different room in which to stay the night. Additionally, the innkeeper refunded the entire amount she had paid for her room, a gesture she appreciated. Although she was apprehensive about another fire in the night, Ahna soon fell asleep.

In the morning, she found Vox, Mikel, and Zavala in the tavern next door, eating a hearty breakfast of sausages and hotcakes. Mikel had cleaned up and shaved, now appearing much more like his normal self. Zavala had been injured in the fire as well, Ahna noted, as attested by the presence of one of Mikel's bandages on her arm. When Ahna questioned her about it, Zavala shrugged it off. "It's no big deal," she explained. "Mikel's just overly cautious."

Pleased to see that all of her friends had made it through the night without further hassle, Ahna settled into breakfast herself. She had suspicions about the source of the previous night's fire but dared not voice them. It had seemed far too co-incidental for a fire to break out near her, just as the fire back in the Academy had done. While she had no fears that someone had set a trap for her in Sapphire, not knowing herself that she would be in this town nor at this particular inn until the moment of decision, it still seemed too much to accept at face value. Much as she wanted to believe otherwise, she was having a difficult time believing that the fires had been anything other than a direct result of her presence. The fact that others had been injured in the fire wounded her far worse than the flames had been capable and she shuddered to think of what may have become of the injured had Mikel not been available to treat their burns.

"I have a favor to ask," Mikel asked once every-one was done eating. "If you don't mind, I would like to stop by the temple this morning before we continue our search. I did a lot of healing last night and I would like to pay tribute and say thanks for the prayers I used on everyone."

"I think that sounds like a wonderful idea," Ahna agreed immediately. She had seen firsthand how useful his abilities had been and, if the shadows under his eyes were any indication, they took quite the toll on him as well. She wondered if that was in any way similar to the way her own powers worked, which required an amount of her personal energy to be extended with every spell cast.

As the group finished their meal and followed Mikel toward the temple, she allowed her mind to wander. Had her questions about the Dark Star been somehow related to the fire? She had to wonder. She suspected it to be the case, as the fire itself hardly seemed accidental. Perhaps he had caught wind of her inquiries and had started the fire in order to stop her meddling. If that truly was the case, she knew, it meant that she was getting close to a discovery... assuming she lived long enough to uncover it.

11

The temple was only a short distance away from the inn. As they approached, Ahna discovered that it was a two-story affair made of stucco and stone, dedicated to the god Pulia'a. Pulia'a was the deity of battle and honorable death, which made Mikel's warhammer a sensible holy symbol. The ground level of the building was completely open, with an assortment of thick but ornately carved supporting columns spaced regularly about, partly for the aesthetic and partly to keep the second floor securely in place. At either end of the building, wide stone stairs led to a balcony that encircled the second floor. The shaded area beneath the bulk of the building was filled with stone-laid walkways, shade bushes, and benches for resting. The garden-like area extended beyond the shadows into the sunlight, where thousands of butterfly-laden flowers bloomed among the greenery. From shrub to flowering shrub, tiny hummingbirds danced, vying with the butterflies for a morning meal of nectar. A low fountain bubbled in the center of the gardens, offering a cool splash for any of the wildlife who cared to drink.

Upstairs and inside, the building was even more beautiful. Pillars, as seen from the exterior, rose through the central chamber and were now sheeted in gold, illuminating the intricate carvings to their fullest. The floor was covered in a star-shaped mosaic with low but well-worn marble steps leading off into antechambers on either side. Overhead, a ceiling made almost entirely of curved stained glass allowed the sun's light to illuminate the room, sending beams of colorful light splaying across the tiles, creating almost as colorful an effect indoors as out. The columns and floor practically glowed from the reflected light in golds, pinks, blues, and greens. At the end of the room, immediately visible to any who entered the chamber, was a blank slate grey wall, its bareness standing in stark contrast to the rest of the building.

It was to this empty wall that Mikel walked,

ignoring the dazzling display of beauty that surrounded him. When he reached the wall, he pulled his warhammer from its holder, held it out before him, bowed his head, and knelt in silent prayer.

Ahna, Zavala, and Vox waited by the entrance while Mikel began his prayers. After only a couple moments, an elderly man dressed in robes similar to those worn by Mikel stepped out of an antechamber and walked over to join them. The only real difference between the two men was about forty years in age and the flail strapped on the elderly cleric's hip in place of Mikel's hammer.

"Vox, it's great to see you again." The approaching cleric reached out an arm and he and Vox clasped wrists in greeting. "How have you been?"

"I've been well, Faegan," Vox smiled as he gripped the head priest's wrist. Only to the massive northman would the man be considered small. "Glad to see you again too."

"What brings you all by today?" He included Ahna and Zavala in his question. "And I see you brought more guests with you as well."

"Mikel did a lot of healing last night over at the inn so he wanted to come by and pay his respects."

Faegan nodded sagely. "I had heard about that.

Terrible news but heartening to hear that nobody died from that fire."

Vox nodded his agreement. "I think that's what he's up there praying about, giving thanks for everyone's lives."

"In that case," Faegan chuckled, "he's going to be there for some time yet. Care for a cup of tea while you wait?" He included Ahna and Zavala in the invitation.

"That would be lovely," Ahna accepted on behalf of everyone. "I'm sure we can all use a drink. My name is Ahna and this is Zavala." She wasn't surprised that Vox had failed to make the introductions already; from what she knew of the northman, he seemed to just assume that everyone already knew each other.

Faegan led the group through an archway on the opposite side of the room, beyond which a small sitting room waited. The sitting room was much more sparsely decorated than the central chamber had been but was comfortable enough. A pair of forest green sofas faced each other, a low table between, with a trio of wooden chairs with padded seats in an arc at one end of the sofas granted plenty of seating for even large groups.

Ahna and Zavala sat on one of the couches, Vox selected the center chair in the trio and Faegan, after setting a steaming pot of tea and five cups onto the table, relaxed into the remaining couch.

After a short while of polite conversation, Ahna explained that she had hired Mikel and Vox as guards to accompany her on her travels. After hearing about the fire at the Academy and discovering the possibility that not only could the Grand Coven but also the assassin known as Dark Star be involved, he let out a low whistle.

"I've heard tell of what kinds of things the Grand Coven has been known to do," Faegan said in a low voice after he took another sip of his tea. "If they are indeed after you, it is a bad thing indeed."

"We're not certain of anything at this point," Zavala was quick to point out. "The rumors at the Academy have been floating around for years and these latest developments, along with Ahna's previous knowledge of the Coven's activities, may just be coincidental." She glanced from Faegan to Ahna before continuing. "We haven't even been able to confirm that someone is really trying to kill Ahna, but we do know that someone killed her family so there's a reasonable suspicion there. We just don't know for sure who was responsible for that."

"That is true," Faegan agreed. "But I have never put much stock into the idea of coincidence. In my experience, as in my teachings, I have come to learn that many things are less coincidental than they appear on the surface, that sometimes when we experience something that we chalk up to co-incidence or other happenstance, it is actually an attempt at communication by the gods, trying to make us understand and recognize that something is important." He took another sip of his tea and settled the cup back onto the table before continu-ing. "Often those messages are simply overlooked in the business of day-to-day life but, for those who are aware, messages can be found everywhere."

"You think that means this coven thing really is trying to kill Ahna?" Vox asked, amazed. "We didn't really think they were truly after her." He looked over at Ahna sheepishly. "Well, maybe Mikel did. I just thought you were scared to be out on your own and wanted someone to help you get back to familiar lands."

"Understandable," she replied. "You didn't really have much reason to suspect that there was much beneath the surface when I hired the both of you." The priest's words echoed her own thoughts, causing her to wonder whether she had put too little stock in her own suspicions.

"Perhaps members of this coven are following Ahna in the hopes of making another attempt on her life," the cleric agreed, "but also perhaps not. You also mentioned the assassin, correct?" When Ahna nodded, he continued. "It seems that your family has a lengthy history of interactions with deadly people. This may just be a symptom of that coexistence or it may be indicative of something yet to come."

Zavala let out a loud guffaw at his statement. "You really think that she," she jutted a finger toward her friend, "is for some reason connected to not just one but two of the most powerful forces in the empire?" She grinned at Ahna. "I mean, sure, there is rumored Grand Coven activity in the Dracott Empire, so it makes sense to connect you there, but the Dark Star? That doesn't even make any sense. Even if he did kill your father – which I'm still not sure I believe – why would he come after you? He doesn't even operate in the Dracott Empire."

"Of course I do not believe that Ahna is connected to two powerful forces in her homeland," Faegan answered with a smile. "I believe that she is somehow connected to three, at the very least."

Now it was Ahna's turn to be shocked. "Three? Where is the third?" The idea of being somehow connected to the Grand Coven, although disconcerting, wasn't altogether unexpected, as her relationship with Zavala alone qualified for that relationship. Much as she hated the idea, the indicated relationship between herself and the Dark Star was also confirmed, assuming that he had indeed been responsible for her father's death. But that only counted as two forces; she was unable to determine from where Faegan had drawn the third. Was there some additional hidden force of which she had been unaware? Was the cleric trying to warn her of some unknown danger?

He reached out to pat her hand with his own massive one. "I am speaking of your own family, of course." He smiled reassuringly. "You are the Countess de Melville, are you not?"

"I... what?" She sat back, blinking without knowing how to answer. "Of course not, why would you think that?" His words made no sense; she wasn't a countess.

"I knew your father," Faegan sat back and poured more tea for everyone. "He was a good man and, despite the changes you have made to your appearance, you look just like him." He sat back against the cushioned backrest of the couch. "With his passing, and those of your mother and brother of course, you are the sole remaining heir to the de Melville name and title that is bestowed alongside it. That makes you a Countess."

For as much time as she had spent reminding herself that she was the last member of her immediate family, Ahna hadn't even considered that she had inherited her father's title upon his death. While she had known that the title would eventually pass from his hands when he passed from this world, it had always been understood that the title would pass to her brother. Although Ahna was the eldest, she was a girl and the title automatically went to the eldest son. She had never entertained the possibility that her beautiful younger brother, the best friend she had ever had throughout her life, would pass before her, that she would truly be the last of her family line. The sofa, the floor, the temple, her entire world shifted beneath her as comprehension settled in her mind. She squeezed her eyes closed, willing the stinging sensation growing there and the tightness in her chest to cease.

As she worked to collect herself and keep the threatening tears from falling, Mikel walked in to join them. Gauging the situation, he silently poured himself a cup of tea and took a seat next to Ahna on the couch. "Has something else happened?" he finally inquired. His voice, as always, was calm and comforting. "Are you all right?"

"She just realized she's a countess," Vox explained when Ahna was unable. "Apparently she hadn't yet made that connection."

"It's so much worse than I thought," she said finally, her vision still blurry and her throat thick with emotion. "I grew up knowing that there was the possibility of danger, everyone in my family knew that. It's why I used a different name while at the Academy," she directed the last statement to Zavala. "Nobody was supposed to know who I was so that I couldn't be used as leverage against my father, against my family. But now with him gone,

I'm no longer a target for leverage. This makes me a target for position."

"Oh, Ahna," Zavala wrapped her arms around her friend and pulled her in close to comfort her. "You don't have anything to worry about. Nothing's going to happen to you as long as we're around."

"She's right," Vox agreed. "We said we'd protect you and we meant it."

"I have something that may help," Faegan added. "Please wait here for just a moment." He stood and walked out of the room. He was only gone a few moments before returning with a small pouch. He handed the pouch to Ahna and sat back to pour himself another cup of tea.

More curious than anything else, Ahna accepted the pouch and untied it, peering inside to see what it held. Not immediately understanding, she reached inside and withdrew a small silver charm, suspended from a delicate matching chain. "Thank you for this," she said to the cleric. "It's lovely."

"Indeed it is," he agreed with a chuckle, "but that's not all it is. It holds a powerful protection enchantment, designed to augment its owner's own personal shields." He stopped laughing and his face turned serious as he added, "I may not truly understand what kinds of dangers you will face but I am certain that this will help to keep you safe. I just hope you don't need it anytime soon."

More appreciative than words could effectively express, Ahna looked at the charm in wonder. It was shaped to form an elaborated knot-like shape, as though the metal itself had been twisted and tied into a complicated twist, one that vaguely appeared like a three-petaled flower with slightly rounded lobes. With trembling fingers, she secured the chain around her neck, tucking the charm itself securely beneath her clothing.

Lost in her own thoughts and the looming realization of just how much waited ahead of her, Ahna paid little attention to the remainder of the conversation. Instead, she sat in silence, holding her cup of tea and staring into its depths. Her own reflection stared back at her, a person she hardly recognized beneath her disguise, until her vision blurred and the image faded into a smear of dark and light colors. To their credit, everyone else seemed to realize that she needed the time to process everything and let her ponder in peace.

Only a short amount of time later, the group found themselves back out in the town square, where they discussed what their next move would be. "It's obvious we can't stay in Sapphire," Ahna explained, her mind still unsettled from the morning's conversation. "If the fire at the inn last night is any indication, the wrong people already know we're here and I don't want to put any more lives in danger than I have to."

She still wasn't entirely sure who the wrong people who had found her were but nevertheless there was danger, even more so for the unsuspecting people who surrounded her. She needed to take steps to protect those she could. If anyone else ended up harmed because she stayed in town longer than she already had, she wasn't sure she would be able to forgive herself. She was having difficulty enough releasing herself from blame for the people who had been injured in the fire, even though she knew there was no way she could have prevented it.

"What about the information you're looking for?" Vox inquired. "Did you already find what you needed?"

Ahna shook her head sadly. "I'm not sure I will

be able to find any more information than what I already have. Much as I would like to continue searching for answers here, I know that the longer we stay, the more danger will appear."

"Do you think the Grand Coven followed you here?" Zavala asked, her eyes wide.

"I really don't know," Ahna admitted. "It might have been them who set the fire last night. I doubt they were responsible, as it seems like a bit of a stretch to believe they would chase me all the way here, but I have to accept that it is a possibility." She looked upwards, where threatening clouds had begun to gather, and then toward the horizon, where the evening fog had begun to creep toward the city. It had been a long time since she had seen such foreboding weather this late in the season and hoped it wasn't an omen of hardships yet to come.

"What about that assassin you were looking into?" Mikel asked. "Did you find what you needed about him?"

Droplets of rain darkened the shoulders of his cloak and the group began to move quickly, heading for shelter as they figured out their next move. The small group ducked into the closest tavern they could find, which was quiet before the evening's festivities. They took a table near the entrance where they could keep a watch, both at the weather and at any who showed more than a passing interest in their small group.

"I already knew quite a lot about him," Ahna explained. "He's been active up north for a long time, so most of the ranking families have at least a passing familiarity with him and his reputation. I think that, assuming the fire last night wasn't an accident, he would be the most likely cause."

Zavala's eyes widened at the idea. "You really think that the Dark Star was at the inn, that he tried to kill you last night?"

"No," Ahna was quick to answer with a wry chuckle. "Of course not. If he had tried to kill me, I wouldn't be here right now to talk about it. If anything, it was a warning for me to stop searching for information about him. If that's the case, it's a warning I intend to heed." While she hadn't been able to come up with any viable ideas on who may have sent the Dark Star after her, still not positive he had been responsible, she wasn't foolish enough to be mistaken on that point. If the notorious assassin wanted her out of Sapphire, she would comply. But the amount of time that had passed between the deaths of her family and the attempts on her person made his involvement seem less likely by the day. That was of little comfort, as she realized the truth behind her conclusions. If Dark Star wasn't trying to kill her but someone else was, she had no idea from which direction the next attack would come.

As the rain increased in intensity, Ahna couldn't keep the sensation of dread from crawling up her spine. Just as the falling rains obscured her vision so that she could no longer see the town square clearly, all of the thoughts whirling through her mind obscured her vision so that she couldn't see the path she needed to take clearly either. Almost involuntarily, her hand raised to the silver knot that Faegan had given her. She hoped she wouldn't need its additional protection any time soon but had serious doubts as to the duration of her own safety.

"You're giving up, then?" Vox asked, confusion apparent in his voice.

"For now, at least," she agreed. Much as she loved the city and wanted to continue her hunt for answers, the longer she stayed in Sapphire, the more danger would appear. If it had been the Dark Star who set fire to the inn, he wasn't likely to just let her hang around and continue being a nuisance. The same logic applied to anyone else who may be currently targeting her.

"I think we should go back to Three Rivers," Zavala suggested. "That's about the last place anyone would expect us to go and we may be able to find more answers while there."

Ahna wasn't sure she agreed with her friend's assessment, still worried about what would happen if she was found. "Just because I am dropping my search for Dark Star, that doesn't mean I am just throwing all caution to the winds. If the Grand Coven really has infiltrated the Academy, that's the last place I should go. I don't know who I can trust there and who I can't, so until I know more, I intend to avoid it."

"That makes sense. Any ideas on where you would like to go, then?"

More townspeople, equally eager to avoid the downpour, shuffled into the tavern. Soon, it was as bustling with activity as any tavern Ahna had ever seen. Instead of increasing her anxiety over her situation, as Ahna had suspected being surrounded by people would have done, she felt a sense of relief. Even with everything that was happening, and would likely continue to happen, life would continue. People would gather, people would celebrate, people would drink to avoid the weather. The same was true no matter where she was, so she may as well go somewhere she enjoyed being.

"How about Aquos?" Ahna suggested after a moment's thought. "It's been many years since I've been, so nobody would think to look for me there." She figured that the last place one would expect to find a group of people on the run, it would be the tropical resort island. If she was to be continuously assaulted by someone whose preferred weapon was fire, she could think of no better place than an island surrounded by water.

"We haven't been there before," Mikel's eyes lit up at the prospect. "Heard a lot of nice things about it but never had the opportunity."

"It's beautiful," Ahna said, her eyes shining. "Plus, my family has friends on the island, so some of them just might know something that they would be willing to share with me."

"Sounds like we have a plan," Mikel said. Everyone agreed so they headed in a hurry, cloaks and other items held over their heads to shield them from the worst of the rain, for the lower levels of town where the docks waited, seeking a ship to take them to paradise.

12

Aquos was every bit as beautiful as Ahna remembered from childhood. The storm that had threatened them as they left Sapphire quickly fell behind them until it was nothing more than a distant memory. Beneath an impossibly azure sky, miles upon miles of pure white sand encircled the island, interrupted only by the occasional coconut palm tree. A warm, gentle, salt-tinged sea breeze blew across the beach, ruffling the leaves of the palms overhead and carrying with it the inherent promises of serenity and peace. Crystal-clear aquamarine water danced along the shoreline, darkening to a deep, rich blue a short distance away from land. The smooth expanse of sea was marked only by the reefs of coral and the occasional school of rainbow-hued fish who flocked to the island by the hundreds, countless varieties of exquisitely-shaped figures beneath the glassy water. There was no sign of the colony of merfolk who were rumored to live below the waves, not that Ahna was surprised. She had heard tell of the merpeople of Aquos her whole life and had never seen so much as a glimpse of any of them in all of the years she and her family had vacationed on the island.

Wooden walkways led out into the water, sun-bleached boards worn smooth through the passage of feet and the occasional storm, leading to a row of cabanas, small buildings with thatched rooves where guests could lounge in the comfort of shade with no interruptions to their relaxation. More cabanas waited further inland, larger spaces that guests could rent for overnight or longer stays. Since they weren't certain how long they would be on the island, the group had rented one of the larger cabanas for three days with an option to stay longer if needed. Since the busy tourism season had not yet started, they had their choice of locations.

"I didn't realize how badly I had needed this," Ahna sighed as she settled into the warm, comforting sand, digging her toes into the warm softness, which wrapped around her in a sun-heated embrace. The sand had absorbed the sunlight as it beamed down from the sky, which it passed along to her in soft waves of heat which entered her skin and flowed all the way into her very soul.

"You said your family comes here all the time?" Zavala asked as she settled into the sand next to her. "I am so jealous!" She flopped backwards, sending a small spray of sand in all directions and sighed in contentment. "I think this is what the heavens must feel like."

"Too hot," Vox said, although the complaint was half-hearted at best. His people hailed from the far north so he was much more comfortable in colder climates, ones filled with slopes of snow and ice-hardened lakes. Tropical islands such as Aquos weren't often high on their lists of places to visit. He raised a hand to shield his eyes from the sun and scanned the beach. "But the water looks nice. Is okay to swim in it?"

"Of course it is," Ahna laughed at the large man's discomfort. "Just about anything is allowed here, so long as you aren't interrupting anyone else's vacation."

Her words weren't simply meant as reassurance.

Aquos was known as the island of hospitality, so the rules upon island guests were few and far between. To Ahna's knowledge, just about any activity was allowed within the confines of the island and the strip of sea that surrounded it. So long as nobody complained about the activities, they were probably allowed. Ostensibly to keep the peace but mostly for the guests' peace of mind, the island housed a small police force, tasked with maintaining a quiet, restful community. Those who caused problems or who became too rowdy were encouraged to calm down. Those who refused to comply or who got out of hand were evicted from the island, some never allowed to return. The trade-off for the relaxed lifestyle allowed on Aquos had seemed optimal for some criminals over the years, criminals who had quickly learned that the small police force on Aquos had neither sympathy nor consideration for their excuses when they got out of hand. Those who remained calm and peaceful were allowed to stay but those who couldn't resist the opportunities offered by the island's wealthy clientele were encouraged to leave the island immediately and had never been allowed to return. Soon, word had spread that while outlaws were allowed on the island, their opportunities for mischief were limited.

Needing no further encouragement, Vox stripped to his undergarments and jogged toward the gently beckoning surf. It appeared that Mikel was about to join him but he stopped, raising a hand to shade his eyes as he scanned the horizon. Following his gaze, Ahna noticed a ship, barely visible in the distance, heading towards Aquos.

"Do you recognize that ship?" she asked, curious about his reaction. He didn't seem overly worried, so she wasn't concerned yet. She also figured the question was superfluous, as there was no way to identify a ship that far in the distance.

"Not sure yet," he admitted, "but that looks a lot like a ship a friend of mine works on. If that's the case, I'll want to go catch up with him for a few moments after they arrive."

The group continued to lounge in the sand and play in the surf while both Mikel and Ahna kept a watchful eye on the ship as it grew closer. As it approached, it was revealed to be a deep maroon in color and much larger than most of the other pleasure boats that had occasionally appeared in their view. A beautiful woman stretched out before the inbound vessel, to which Ahna had to raise approving eyebrows. Ships with figureheads were uncommon and this one was particularly lovely.

"That's the Temptress, all right," Mikel said as it grew ever closer. "Flagship of a trading company based in the Inland Sea, not too far away from Three Rivers. You don't have to worry, though," he was quick to reassure the woman in the sand next to him. "There's nobody harmful on that boat. At least, nobody that you need to worry about." He chuckled and added, "you may need to watch out for Dane, though. That boy has an eye for the ladies, particularly lovely young ones such as yourself."

They continued to watch as the Temptress pulled into harbor. Once it docked, men and women began flooding off the boat, most of whom only made it as far as the white sand beach before throwing themselves to the ground in a similar manner to the way that Ahna and Zavala had done.

Once all of the crew had debarked, Mikel pushed himself to his feet and brushed the bulk of sand away from his clothing. "I see Cookie," he said. "He's the friend I mentioned. I'll stay within view, so you will be perfectly safe." His expression was serious as he looked over at where Ahna lay. His gaze traveled from her to the edge of the water, where the scantily-clad man hunted for shells in the shallow depths. "Vox will stay here also, just to be extra sure."

"I'm sure we'll be fine," she reassured him. "Go visit with your friend. I'm going to head into town myself fairly shortly to look for a friend of mine as well. We'll meet back up right here when we're both done, so have a good time."

While Aquos was most known for its beaches, there was a tiny village nestled into the center of the island. This village wasn't just a place for those who worked the beachside area to live and raise their own families, it also housed a handful of small shops, which offered a dizzying array of sea- and beach-themed goods. Jewelry fashioned from shells and corals, dishes carved from coconut husks, goggles that had been specially designed for seeing below the water, colorful bathing suits, plush towels for lying on and drying off with, and anything else a visitor could possibly want could be found by those who took a short stroll through a wide, well-kept path from the beaches and into the palms. Wide-bloomed red, yellow, white, and pink flowers lined the path and grew throughout the village, leaving a light, sweet scent everywhere.

After only a few minutes, Ahna discovered that her family's friends, who she had hoped to meet up with while on the island, weren't available. They had left for the off season, so she contented herself with what little bit of exploration was available. Most of the trinkets were of little interest to her outside their obvious aesthetic value, so as much as she would have enjoyed purchasing an assortment of small trinkets for her travelling companions and her friends back home, she knew that she still needed to save what little funds she still had. Once her current set of problems ended, she was sure, she could return and do some leisurely shopping.

She soon found herself back on the shaded but deeply-scented pathway leading to the beach. Before getting more than a few steps away from the village, however, she overheard a familiar voice. Curious, she turned around to follow the sound to its source.

She found Mikel, sitting on the floor of a tiny

hut with an elderly man. The man appeared to be in his fiftieth year of age, if not more.

Spotting her, Mikel waved her over. "Cookie, this is Ahna," he made introductions. "Cookie is the head chef on the Temptress, that ship that just pulled in."

Ahna was visibly surprised at his words. She never would have imagined that a man in his advanced age would still be working, let alone in an environment as dangerous as that on a ship. Not that she would say anything about it, of course. "It's a pleasure to meet you," she said graciously as she stepped up to join them. "I didn't mean to intrude."

"Not at all," Cookie waved her objections away. "I adore meeting new people." He patted the seat next to him, a clear indication of invitation.

Seeing no real reason to continue resisting, Ahna accepted his invitation. "What's it like to work on a big ship like that?" she inquired. Although she and her family had been on a great number of ships, she'd had very little interaction with the crew while they had been aboard. She was naturally curious, so this opportunity to speak with someone from a completely different world than that which she knew was not one she was about to pass up. Particularly, it seemed, when it was someone that Mikel appeared to trust. She had seen no reason to refute his judgement so far, so there was no reason to distrust Cookie now.

"Not much different from working anywhere else, I suppose," Cookie said with a chuckle. "Other than the floor moving about under you a bit more on the ship than it generally does on land." After that, his face turned serious. "I'm very sorry to hear about what happened to your father. He was a good man."

Surprise widened her eyes at his words and she glanced back and forth between the men, wondering if she had miscalculated on where to place her trust. "You know who I am?"

"Of course. Your eyes are unmistakable. In fact, I met you once before, although you were still a small child at that point." He smiled at her reassuringly, a hint of sadness at the edges of his eyes.

"I'm sorry, I don't remember."

"Not to worry. As I said, you were young. He used to come into my restaurant all the time, brought you with him a few times. He just loved the painted crab and you thought the colors on the crab shells were pretty."

She could picture the image of herself and her father, sharing a meal and commenting on the crab shells. It sounded very much like similar memories she still had of time spent with the man. "You had a restaurant too?"

"Still do," he chuckled. "My wife and kids manage the place while I'm out on the boat."

"We were talking about the fire in Sapphire," Mikel explained. "You had also mentioned a fire at the Academy while you were there, correct?" When Ahna agreed, he continued. "We've been assuming that these are connected but are you really sure that the Dark Star is behind both of them?"

"Not entirely," she admitted. "I suspected that the fire in Sapphire was because I was looking for information on him but, outside of what happened with my family, there wasn't much of a reason for him to start the fire at the Academy. And the only reason he would have to target me would be if someone hired him to do so, and there really isn't much reason to do that." She looked between the men. "Regardless of who my father was or whether he was supposed to inherit the throne, that honor would never pass to me without a direct decision by Emperor du Toit. It wouldn't be handed down to me from my father at all."

"It's interesting," Cookie said thoughtfully. "We're based out of Hoem, which is near Three Rivers. I would have expected to have heard something about a fire there but there's been no mention of it."

"The Magi are probably keeping it pretty quiet," Ahna added. "It wouldn't look good for news of a fire to spread. People might decide to attend a different academy instead of the one in Three Rivers." Then she remembered something that the Magi had said just after the fire had been put out. "It was reported as an accident," she said. "The Magi didn't want anyone to grow suspicious about what had happened there, so they just referred to it as an accident, caused by one of the younger students." She couldn't remember all of the details, but that was at least the gist of what she remembered.

Cookie and Mikel both nodded at the idea. "People don't want to learn where they aren't safe."

"Mikel also mentioned the Grand Coven," Cookie said. "Sounds like a pretty dangerous bunch of people. I haven't heard anything of this group on my own but I will take the information to our loremaster. If anyone knows something about them, its Wyrm."

"I'd really appreciate that." With all of the events that had been happening, Ahna hadn't forgotten about the threat posed by the Grand Coven but she had started to question whether they were truly involved in anything either, just as she had begun to question the involvement of the Dark Star. She still wasn't sure how either the assassin or the Grand Coven fit into the things that kept happening around her, if they did at all.

On the other hand, if she was being as cautious as she should, she also had to admit that she was starting to suspect that, just perhaps, there was much more of a connection among all of the pieces involved than she had previously considered. There was a chance, albeit a slight one, that the assassin himself was a member of the Coven. If he had magical powers, that could explain how he was able to do all of the things to which he had been accredited. She couldn't imagine anything more dangerous than a highly skilled assassin who also knew the magical arts.

She briefly considered sharing her suspicions with Mikel and Cookie but decided against it. There was no reason to concern them with her latest round of wild speculation and, if things turned out to be nothing as she hoped they would, she wouldn't have to face any questions from them either.

Zavala wasn't feeling hungry when dinnertime rolled around. "Probably just a little too much sun when I'm not used to it," she explained. "I think I'll just stay here, if you guys are okay with that. I'll get some sleep while you guys are gone and hopefully feel better when you get back."

"Okay." Ahna wasn't sure that leaving Zavala all alone when she wasn't feeling well but once Mikel assured her that there was nothing seriously wrong with her friend, she acquiesced. Perhaps Zavala was just feeling overwhelmed with everything, or maybe she just needed a break from the group. Either way, Ahna was willing to comply. "If you need anything," she said before they left, "just send word to us and we'll be back before you know it."

The trio had only just settled down at a table in the bustling beachside café before familiar faces began to appear. "Cookie!" Mikel greeted his friend. "Won't you join us?"

"Be glad to," Cookie accepted, introducing his companion as he pulled out a chair. "Nice to see you again, Ahna, and you as well, Vox. This is Wyrm, I mentioned him earlier."

"Your loremaster," Mikel agreed. "It's a pleasure."

The loremaster was easily old enough to be Cookie's father and Ahna wondered what it was about the man who kept him so spry at his advanced age. The years had taken most of his hair but what was left was as white as the sands and as thin as a whispered rumor.

Wyrm harrumphed and barely glanced among the trio. "I take it you are the ones that's making this one pester me so much?" He jabbed a thumb in Cookie's general direction but accepted the offered seat. "He's been asking me about a lot of things lately, on your behalf I surmise." His voice was far stronger than his appearance would suggest, with almost no sign of his advanced age.

Mikel looked like he was about to speak but Ahna beat him to it. "That's correct," she agreed.

"We're sorry to be such a bother but if you do have any information, we'd be happy to hear it."

Wyrm finally turned to face her fully, eyeing her critically with sharp eyes as he did so. "Don't look much like someone who'd be interested in the Grand Coven." He settled into his seat and stretched, a series of loud popping sounds emanating from his back as he did. "But then, I suppose looks always have been deceiving, now haven't they?"

She smiled sweetly at the ancient man. "That may be so," she agreed, "but nevertheless we'd like to know anything you can tell us. We will cover your dinner, of course, for the hassle." She included Cookie in her invitation, which was abruptly waved away by Wyrm.

"Never sell information," he said. "Its bad luck, I tell ya. Best if you remember that, all of you." He included Ahna, Vox, Mikel, and even Cookie in the last statement.

"Sorry, I hadn't meant to offend."

"Don't mind him," Cookie reassured her with a chuckle. "Wyrm thinks that everything is bad luck nowadays."

Wyrm harrumphed again, whether in agreement or not she couldn't tell. "That's because you guys seem to go out of your way to look for trouble. Even now, you're scooping up every bit of it that you can find and bringing all of the bad luck home with you."

"About the coven," Vox interrupted before Wyrm could get started on what was appearing to be a well-rehearsed argument, "we have reason to believe that one or more members of the coven might be targeting us."

"Might 'a been," Wyrm agreed, "or might not. Can't say as I know anything about their motivations but I can tell ya what I do know about them.

"They're a secretive bunch, likes to keep to themselves more'n most. They've been keeping to themselves a long time now, long enough that most people don't think that they're anything more than tall stories to frighten people."

"Do you think they're just legends, then?" Mikel leaned forward with the question, curiosity drawing him in closer.

"Course not," the aged loremaster harrumphed again. "Wouldn't 'a bothered even telling you if I thought that. Nope, they're real, all right. Now that's a good-looking fish if ever I saw one." He leaned forward and sniffed as his meal was placed before him. He waited for the server to leave and took a healthy bite, chewing slowly with obvious delight as he savored the meal, before continuing. "Like I said, they're a secretive group, so it's hard to really know what they're up to. They draw a handful of aspiring mages from the Academy in Three Rivers, I assume you all know where that is, as well as some of the other academies throughout the empire. Last I heard, they were spread pretty much everywhere from the Dracott Empire, down through the Sapphire Empire, and over into the Inland Empire. 'Bout the only place they haven't gotten into much yet is the Barberry Empire. Not sure why, probably on account o' the cold there. Don't think they've gone too much west of Sapphire or east of Inland Sea but it's possible they have and I just hadn't heard anything about it yet." With emphasis, he stabbed his fork into his meal again, chewing for a moment in silent contentment.

"Why are they looking for mages in training?" Ahna asked. "Wouldn't it make more sense for them to seek out mages who have already been trained?"

"That would be a line of thinking, sure enough. But by the time most mages finish their training, they're already getting established. No, what these guys want is younger, impressionable folk who they can guide into the paths they want 'em in. I don't know just how many they've gotten to so far but I do know they've been putting their people into positions of power throughout the three empires for years."

"What are they trying to do?" Ahna asked, appalled at what the man was saying. If even half of his information was correct, she was in even more danger than she had initially thought. Having people in power in the Dracott, Sapphire, and Inland Empires, people who were ultimately controlled by the Grand Coven, was a terrible idea. She didn't even want to consider what kinds of damage they could cause with that level of political power. If they did manage to get a foothold in the Barberry Empire as well, that would be exponentially worse.

"No idea," Wyrm admitted. "Whatever it is that they're after though, it can't be good. Nobody spends that long and puts that much effort into building up a secret group like that, putting people into strategic places, without having one monster of an end goal. If it was for something good, word would'a leaked out by now. People like to talk about the things they do, particularly when they expect to get praised for it, you know?"

"Yeah, I think that makes a lot of sense," Mikel agreed. His expression had grown more and more concerned as Wyrm had continued to talk. One hand wrapped around his warhammer, likely an unconscious move on his part but one that didn't go unmissed by other members of the group. Thankfully, none of them commented on his posture.

Wyrm set his fork down on his plate with a loud clatter. "If you intend to keep investigating these people," he cautioned, "be careful. Be more than careful, be the careful-est you've ever been. Others have gone digging into this group, others who were far more prepared than what you guys seem to be, never ended well for 'em."

"What do you mean?" Vox inquired. "What happened to them?"

"Most of 'em just disappeared. Never heard from again. Those, you see, those was the lucky ones."

"How could disappearing be considered lucky?" The familiar creeping sensation along her spine returned, reaching almost all the way up to her hairline as she considered the possibilities.

"Normally it's not," Wyrm agreed. "But compared to what happened to those who were found, just being gone is a blessing. Bad enough having to find out your loved ones is gone, even worse to discover your loved ones is used as components."

Ahna blinked rapidly, not sure that she had heard that correctly. "Components?" she repeated. "You mean, like spell components?"

"Sure 'nuff," the loremaster agreed. "You probably know that most of the animals out there can be used as components for different spells, most people know about that. But what most people don't realize, unless they have a darned good reason to, is that people aren't any different. End of the day, we're all animals, just a bit smarter than other ones like this fish here. We can all be used for spell components, but a body has to be pretty darned evil to use us like that."

The group sat in stunned silence, digesting both the meal and the words that had just been shared. Ahna felt slightly nauseated just thinking about the idea of humans being used as spell components, or any of the other races for that matter. Despite her disgust, she knew that Wyrm's words were true. Almost any spellcaster worth their training robes understood that an evil mage could use humans in such a manner, even if it was never openly discussed. She simply hadn't ever seriously considered the idea of actually using people as components.

"There were a couple other things that were asked about." Obviously sensing the distress in the group, Wyrm changed the subject. "I heard you guys were looking for more information on the Dark Star also. Why is that? Seems to me like looking for an assassin like 'im is almost as dangerous as looking into the Coven."

Ahna nodded, still not certain that her dinner would stay in place. She swallowed hard in an attempt to dislodge the knot in her throat. "I have reason to believe he killed Count de Melville up in the Dracott Empire, possibly even killed his whole family. I thought there might be some sort of a connection there."

"Naw," Wyrm harrumphed again as he pushed his chair back and heaved himself to his feet. "He had nothing to do with that. I heard the same rumors as you did but there's no truth to 'em."

"How can you be so sure?" Mikel pressed for more details.

"Because the Dark Star was nowhere near the Dracott Empire when the Count was killed."

Ahna blinked in surprise. Of all the things the loremaster had said, that was almost as shocking as his statements about the missing people who had been searching for the Grand Coven. "How do you know that?" she asked. "How do you know he wasn't there? Do you know who he is?" The idea that the loremaster could have uncovered the assassin's identity had never crossed her mind, which led her to realize that she needed to start thinking about things a lot more clearly if she wanted to stop being taken by surprise at almost every conversation she had.

Wyrm laughed aloud at the absurdity of her question. "D'ye think that anybody who uncovers the identity of the most dangerous assassin in these here empires gets to live to tell of it? Of course not. All's I know is that he was busy elsewhere while Count de Melville was getting killed."

"But what about the Grand Coven?" Despite

her earlier hesitance to do so, Ahna described her idea that the assassin may be part of the Coven, using magic to stay hidden from view. "Is he a part of that too?"

"Nope," Wyrm said as he walked away from the table. "There's no way the Dark Star'd be caught up in something like that. And if he knew you was thinking so," he looked back over at the group, making eye contact with each of them in turn, "he'd be mighty upset to hear about it."

13

"I think I need to talk to Zavala," Ahna said quietly once Cookie and Wyrm were gone. "We're really not making a lot of progress this way and she's the only real resource I 've got left to figure out what is going on."

"Why Zavala?" Vox asked. "Just because she's been training longer?"

"No, that's not it. She said that her mother was a part of the Grand Coven, remember?" Ahna was tired of being shocked at everything she heard. She needed answers, and she needed them now. Every time she had asked about Zavala's mother, her friend had quickly changed the subject. No big surprise, as Ahna could understand her reticence to discuss their relationship, but she had run out of options. If the only way she had to get any real information was to interrogate her best friend, she would just have to live with the consequences. Zavala had information she needed and Ahna was determined to get it from her, regardless of how uncomfortable it made both of them.

"Right, I had forgotten about that."

They headed back down the beach toward their cabana. Heading inside, Ahna was once again surprised, this time at the discovery that her friend was nowhere to be found. She walked back outside and circled the miniature building, following the wooden porch that surrounded the cabana but there was no sight of Zavala. "What happened to her?" she asked, her voice trembling with concern.

"Let's go see if we can find her," Mikel suggested. "Perhaps she started to feel better and came to join us for dinner and we just missed each other somehow."

Although she had little faith in Mikel's suggestion, understanding that it was less intended as a real idea of what had happened to Zavala and more as a suggestion for them to stay calm and hopeful that Zavala was fine, Ahna agreed and the group headed out to search along the beach and nearby forested areas.

The moon rose full and swollen overhead and the sands, almost blindingly white in the sunlight, now sparkled in the moon's reflected glory. Waves crashed gently ashore, waiting for the shifting tides and carrying the scent of the ocean, tangy with salt. The trio combed every portion of the island they could find but there was no sign of Zavala. The island was not very large and the small group was easily able to search it in only a few hours. Finally having to admit defeat as the rising sun began to hint at the horizon, they returned to the cabana, exhausted.

Ahna fell onto the bed that she had been sharing with Zavala, curled up into a ball, and willed herself to sleep. Although she clung to the hope that her spunky friend was safe and healthy, wherever she was, doubts crowded into her mind. How many more people, those dear to her, would be lost before this was all over?

Her pillow was still damp when she woke later that morning but Ahna ignored it. She had more important things to worry about than a soggy pillow. The bed that Vox and Mikel had been sharing was empty, blankets piled in a heap in the center of the mattress. Their boots and Mikel's warhammer were gone as well, which gave Ahna some re-assurance that they hadn't simply disappeared in the night. Wherever the men were, she was sure they were okay.

As she secured the last button on her boots, she heard the faint sound of conversation drifting in from outside. Curious, she stepped quietly to the door to listen. Her eyes widened as she recognized the voices.

"Zavala!" she cried as she burst through the door, almost tripping over Vox in her haste to reach her friend. "We looked everywhere, where were you? I thought something awful had happened to you!"

"Whoa, calm down there, Ahna," Zavala laughed as she caught the excited girl. "I'm fine; I didn't mean to worry anyone."

"But where were you?"

"I went out to the beach to soak up a little bit of the sun before it went down," she explained. "I thought it might make me feel a little better. But I guess I fell asleep because by the time I woke, it was morning."

"Apparently the sleep helped," Mikel added. "You're looking perfectly healthy today." His voice sounded odd but his posture was relaxed. Most likely, he hadn't slept much better than Ahna had that night.

Zavala nodded. "I didn't want to wake you guys up, so I stayed out here until Mikel and Vox came out just a few minutes ago."

Ahna stood back, relieved to see that all of the fears she had held the previous night had been unfounded. She had already lost too many people, to lose Zavala as well would have been devastating. "I'm so glad to see it."

"Now that we're all up," Mikel suggested, "perhaps breakfast is in order. Let's go see what we can find, then we can decide where to go from here."

"Sounds like a great idea," Ahna said. "I'm famished."

Vox, always in the mood for a hearty meal, readily agreed and the men stepped toward the beach.

"Can you hang back a moment?" Zavala grabbed Ahna lightly by the arm as she passed. "I'd like to talk over a couple things with you privately, if you don't mind."

"Not at all." She waved to the men. "You two

go find somewhere good and we'll catch up to you soon."

The morning sun glinted off the water as waves rose and fell. A small trail of footprints, left by one of the sea birds, no doubt, led further up the beach. The scent of the sweet flowers which grew everywhere on the island danced on the breeze. Nearby trees waved lazily, enjoying the breeze as well. The men strode purposefully but without hurry toward the pathway that led deeper into the island, in the direction of the village.

Once the men were out of sight, Zavala pulled Ahna back into the cabana. "We need to go," she explained as she handed Ahna her pack. Her voice was much firmer than Ahna had ever heard it before and no hint of her normal good humor shone in her eyes.

"What's going on?" Ahna asked, confused. She caught her bag as Zavala dropped it into her hands, still trying to make sense of the situation. "Why are you in such a hurry all of a sudden? Why did you wait for them to leave before saying something?" She couldn't understand what was going on or why her friend had suddenly changed from friendly and affable to serious and hurried.

"They're not coming with us," Zavala explained as she pulled Ahna toward the door. "I'd hoped we would be able to escape before they woke up but you were sleeping too deeply and didn't want to wake up when I came in last night."

"Wait a moment." Halfway down the wooden walkway that led from the cabana porch to the beach, Ahna stopped and dug in her heels. "Just… wait. I'm not leaving without them, I brought them with me for a reason. You can't protect me, that's why I hired them."

Zavala turned on her, more serious than Ahna had ever seen the older girl. "No," she said. "Absolutely not. They're staying here and you're coming with me. We're leaving this island right now."

"No, wait," Ahna dug in her heels, trying to make sense of the situation. "I'm not going without them." She had no idea what had changed with her friend, why she was suddenly so determined to remove Ahna from her guards, but she didn't trust it. Despite everything that had happened recently, there had been no reason for her to abandon the men and unless Zavala gave her a good reason why it was necessary, she had no intention of complying. The sudden change in Zavala, on the other hand, gave her grave concerns. She wondered whether it had something to do with the change in Mikel's tone before he and Vox had left. "Did you guys have some sort of argument or something?" While she could understand how that could happen, Zavala was often abrasive when she felt threatened, it still didn't explain her abrupt change in demeanor.

As Ahna tried to maintain her position and sort out what was going on, smoke began to billow up from the sand beneath their feet, slowly coalescing into solid forms. The first for to take on a recognizable shape was a girl about Ahna's age with orange-tipped fingernails. "Kerry?" Ahna whispered as she recognized the girl from her mental arts class. "What are you doing here?"

Kerry didn't bother to answer and was quickly joined by more solidifying shapes. Smoke turned into more people, including a petite, pale-haired girl wearing a sneer and an older woman of about thirty years, her hair pulled back into an ornate braid and woven through with silvery threads.

Other than her previous schoolmate, Ahna had never encountered any of the new women before, at least not that she was aware, but their presence there couldn't mean good news. Kerry's arrival did nothing to reassure her about Zavala's intentions. Quite the opposite, in fact, it confirmed that, whatever her friend was up to, it was not in Ahna's best interests. Her hopes that the change in Zavvie were based on nothing more substantial than a dispute with Vox and Mikel dimmed like a candle snuffed for the night.

"Look," Zavala turned to her, irritation blazing in her eyes. "You have two choices right now. Either you come with us willingly or we take you by force. Either way, you're coming with us right now." She raised her hand and began the series of gestures needed to cast a spell.

Ahna could feel every beat of her heart as Zavala spoke. Time stood still for the briefest of moments but an eternity at the same time. Small, colorful birds erupted soundlessly from the bushes that lined the beach, disappearing into the island's depths. While her mind heard and comprehended every syllable her friend said, every person who appeared around her, her heart refused to accept them. This couldn't be happening. Zavala was her closest friend, the person she loved as much as she loved her own family. How could she do this to her?

Even as she tried to make sense of the words echoing in her ears, the first spell hit her. A blast of fire, similar to the searing heat that had filled her dormitory all those weeks previously and the fire that had more recently chased her out of Sapphire, struck her in the chest, knocking her backward. She stumbled but managed to maintain her footing, balanced precariously on the edge of the narrow walkway. "Zavvie," she whimpered, "you're one of them? Why are you doing this to me?"

"The same reason I became your mentor and friend for all these years. You have something we want." What had once been one of the most soothing voices in Ahna's world had turned to steel, hardened edges cutting through every word. "We tried to invite you in to join us but you just wouldn't come along like a good little girl." She stepped closer, nudging Ahna even further up the narrow walkway as she tried to maintain distance between them. "No, instead you had to hire those men to come along on your little journey with you. Do you know how hard it was to get rid of them?"

"None of it was real?"

Zavala laughed. "Did you really think that anyone was interested in being friends with a spoiled brat like you? Of course not. The only reason I even tolerated your presence is because you have power."

"But you have a lot more magic than I do," Ahna protested as she backed towards the cabana. The wooden building wouldn't do much to safeguard against Zavala's flames but hopefully by the time she reached the structure, Ahna would come up with a plan. "You never needed me." She just needed to keep the other girl talking so that she could think.

"Yes, I do have a lot more magic. At least you understand just how overmatched you are right now. But no, what I'm talking about isn't magical power. You're the last heir to the throne."

"The throne?" For a moment, Ahna couldn't figure out what the cruel woman was talking about. "You mean the throne of the Dracott Empire?" Suddenly, Wyrm's warning floated through her memories. Apparently, this was what the loremaster had meant when he said that the Grand Coven was amassing power of all varieties. Her initial suspicions had been correct after all, they really were after her… just not for the reasons she had expected.

"Exactly. Now that we have everyone out of the way, you're the last in line."

"But that's not true," Ahna protested, not that she expected her pursuers to believe her. "Just because my father was supposed to succeed the emperor, that doesn't mean I will." If she could just convince the women that she wasn't next in line for the throne, perhaps there would be a way for her to save herself and escape from whatever plans they had in store for her.

"We've already made arrangements for it to happen," the sneering girl, one of the people who had appeared from the smoke, explained. "Now stop backing away from us and learn how to behave." Her sneer deepened as she added, "a high-born woman such as yourself should have better manners than this."

"Roshlyn, Hethere, grab her." Zavala's voice cut through Ahna's heart as she felt something solid behind her and she knew that she was out of time. Zavala wasn't the only one with spells readied in her direction. Even as Ahna looked at the group of coven members, an assortment of elemental attacks came flying in her direction. Geysers of fire, shards of ice, bolts of electrical energy and even blinding light dazed and confused her. The world began to spin and Ahna stumbled back and forth under the barrage. Every step she took seemed to trigger another attack and finally she slumped against the railing that safeguarded guests from falling off the balcony and into the sea.

She could feel the tattoos across her back as they flared to her defense, sigils her father and a legacy of fathers before him had placed upon her body for just such an occurrence. Ahna had never expected for the greatest and most immediate threat to her personal safety to come from the person she trusted the most.

In an instant, she understood everything.

Whether what she had said about her mother was true or not, the facts staring her in the face were undeniable. Zavala was a member of the Grand Coven.

She had lied to her.

She had lied about everything.

If she didn't escape, Ahna knew that she would be killed. She briefly considered returning the spellcasting challenge but knew that she was drastically outnumbered and outmatched. Even if she did manage to successfully cast a spell against one of them, there was no way to defeat them all. Against one, she had a possibility of victory. Against two, she was unlikely to emerge victorious. Only her sigils would give her an edge, which she didn't think would be enough. Not that it mattered. Against three or more, she stood no chance whatsoever. Their combined might far outmatched her own. She needed to get away from them to somewhere she could be safe. She needed somewhere she could think, plan, come up with a way to get out of the situation alive.

There was nowhere to go and no time to make a plan. A lifetime of training, cautionary tales to keep her on her guard and watchful of an attack had been for naught. She was going to die in paradise, the last hope of the de Melville family, killed by a friend's betrayal and her own folly. The realization shook some of the self-pity from her mind and she heard her father's voice speaking clearly in her mind, telling her to move.

As she had done for every day of her life, she obeyed her father's instructions.

She moved.

Knowing that it was her only chance of survival, Ahna heaved herself to her feet, crying out in pain from the rain of magic that continued to fall over her and dove into the water. Weighted down as she was, she quickly sank to the bottom, which was not nearly as far beneath the surface as she would have liked. Her own blood fogged the water, making it difficult to tell in which direction she should head for cover.

To her amazement, the water itself stayed a few inches away from her body as a pocket of air surrounded her. She wondered whether it was due to one of the spells that had been cast upon her or if it had been triggered by one of her own defenses but lacked the time to find out for certain. Spotting an area that appeared to be slightly darker than the rest of the sea floor, she kicked and swam toward it, hoping she was moving toward safety instead of away from it.

The bubble of air allowed her to breathe, but only shallowly. She understood that her air supply was limited, as she wasn't certain that the air would replenish itself as she swam, but there was no choice in the matter. She could hear the Coven members above, calling to each other as they tried to track her movements.

Think clearly now and come up with a plan. Her father's voice echoed through her mind as she swam parallel to shore, trying to gain as much distance between herself and her attackers as possible. *I can hold my breath for three minutes.* She gauged the size of the bubble that continued to surround her as she moved. *With this air pocket, I will have perhaps five minutes of air.* She knew that swimming cost far more energy than walking and, weighted down as she was, she settled onto the seabed floor. *That means I have eight minutes to survive.* Eight minutes is not a large amount of time. Walking would be slower but she could conserve more energy, making her available air last just a little bit longer. Seconds could mean the difference between safety and death.

Zavvie can fly, she reminded herself, *so she's probably tracking me above water.* Surfacing at any point would immediately draw another attack. She wasn't sure how she would be able to escape the water while she still had air left and avoid her pursuer. The clarity of the water in which she moved didn't help, as she knew she was plainly visible to any who followed her from above. In the distance she could see a large formation in the water, either a shoal of rocks or some sort of tree grove, she wasn't sure. Knowing that was her best opportunity, she headed in that direction.

As she approached, she discovered that neither of her assumptions was correct. What she had initially believed to be rocks or trees turned out to be the underside of a ship. *I must be near the docks.* It was the only place for ships that size to moor safely. Spotting another shaded area beyond the hull, she moved quickly in that direction. Remembering how many dockworkers and vessel crew members were constantly running up and down the docks, she hoped that Zavala wouldn't be so brash as to attack her in full view of so many other people. There was no other choice, she had to breach the surface and replenish her air or die. There were no other options.

The pocket of air that had surrounded her was long since gone and her lungs afire by the time she finally pulled herself, gasping and choking while still trying to remain as silent as possible, to the surface. She looked around hurriedly, shaking the briny water off of her face as she did. There was no sign of Zavala or any of the others who had accosted her at the cabana but it didn't matter. As long as she was on the island, she wasn't safe.

She snuck along the shoreline, careful to watch for any signs of pursuit either on the ground or in the air as she went, until she was certain she had escaped. Finally able to stop and take stock of her situation, she huddled in the center of a small thicket of trees just beyond the ridge of sand, shaking in fear and sobbing from the betrayal she had just experienced. "Why did you do this to me?" she asked the empty air.

As she slowly regained control over herself, she rummaged through her satchel to withdraw a handful of components. She hadn't kept many on her person, not believing she would be required to cast many spells but that morning's experience, brief as it may have been, had taught her a great many things. First and foremost, it had taught her that the spells she knew would be dearly needed if she was to survive and that, in order to cast them, she would need a lot more supplies. Thankfully, she kept a small quantity of basic components on her at all times, just in case an emergency arose.

In her opinion, this qualified as an emergency.

She cast her communication spell, one that every first-year student was required to learn, in order to contact Mikel and Vox. She wasn't entirely sure where the men were currently located and had no interest in opening herself up for another attack by searching for them. "I need you," she whispered into the glowing light cupped in her palms. "Meet me by the docks, please hurry."

"What happened to you?" Mikel's voice, strained with worry, returned from the same ball of light. "You didn't show up for breakfast and when we returned to the cabana, it was on fire. We've been searching everywhere for you, are you okay?"

"I'll tell you all about it," she reassured him, "but for now I'm okay. I just need to get off this island."

"We're on our way."

True to his word, Mikel and Vox arrived at the docks less than a minute later. Worry creased Mikel's face and even stalwart Vox, who had seemed unshakeable throughout this whole ordeal, appeared concerned. Mikel rushed to Ahna's side as soon as she stepped out of the thicket in which she had been hiding. Even as he moved, she could feel his spells washing over her, healing the myriad of small wounds that had continued to bleed, soaking through her clothes.

"I need to get out of here," she explained as she finished the story of the attack at the cabana and Zavala's betrayal.

"Definitely," Vox agreed. "Let's get you to a portal right now. I'll get everyone out of the way so we can get away faster."

"No," Mikel disagreed. "That would be unwise. She found you at the portal in Hub last time so it would be reasonable for her to be expecting us to take the portal again. We need to find a different way out of here, perhaps on board a ship."

"Where do we want to head?" Vox asked as he began walking toward the docks to find them passage.

"Anywhere. Just find us passage on the first ship leaving here."

14

Vox booked the trio passage on the Bullfrog, which was captained by a large, friendly blond man named Dane. Initially, Ahna was concerned about traveling on a ship she didn't know, but both Vox and Mikel quickly reassured her of her safety. "This ship is part of the McClannahan Trading fleet," Vox explained, naming one of the largest and most well-known trading companies in the Inland Empire.

As far as Ahna knew, McClannahan Trading's reach didn't quite extend to the Dracott Empire but it was a well-known and highly respected company. Her father had been seeking the means to begin trading with McClannahan Trading before Ahna had left home but she had no idea what the status of his attempts had been. Perhaps, had he been unable to succeed in that attempt, this could grant her the ability to finish what her father had started, a welcome change. It would be nice to continue her father's work instead of hiding from everything as she had been.

"Same as the Temptress," Mikel added, "the ship that Cookie and Wyrm were on yesterday." Seeing that the assurance helped to make her feel more comfortable with the idea, he continued. "Red John's a real no-nonsense kind of guy. There's no way he'd ever put up with any funny business on any of his ships, so you've got nothing to worry about from any of his men. Even Dane could come to your aid, should you need it. He was a guardian on the Temptress until he took over captainship of the Bullfrog."

"Red John?" She wasn't familiar with the name.

"His actual name's John McClannahan. He's the owner of McClannahan Trading."

"Besides," Vox added, "we're going to be there too. After what your lady friend pulled this morning, we're not leaving your side again."

The knot that had been building up in Ahna's stomach relaxed a bit at their reassurance. Not that she didn't have any reason to distrust Vox and

Mikel, she was still stinging from Zavala's betrayal and not feeling secure in any of her relationships at that moment. However, she understood that she needed to trust someone and the men had given her no reason to doubt them. If anything, their actions so far had given her nothing but reasons to trust them. "Let's go."

The first stop the Bullfrog made was at a tiny town called Dive. The trip was a little shorter than Ahna had realized, so they arrived less than a day after departing from Aquos. That amount of time hadn't been enough for her to gain audience with the captain, to her disappointment. Perhaps she would get another opportunity to try on the next leg of the journey. Or perhaps waiting until her life and the lives of those around her were no longer under immediate threat would be better. There was no imperative for her to develop her network of contacts right at that moment, after all. Assuming she survived, she could always travel back to the Inland Sea and see about building her network of contacts and increasing the family business.

"Doesn't look like much," Ahna remarked as she and her companions walked down the gangplank onto the docks.

Dive appeared similar to most of the other coastal towns in that area, blazingly hot but without the cool breezes that made Aquos such a desirable location. Despite being on the shores of the Azul Sea, the air still managed to be thick and heavy. Less than an hour after their arrival, Ahna's clothes had become stuck fast to her skin. There were an assortment of shops offering all manner of freshly caught sea life which would have been otherwise tempting but Ahna had other interests.

"Never been here before? We have, about a year ago. What are you looking for?" Mikel asked as Ahna left yet another shop without selecting any purchases. "Maybe we can help you find what you need."

"Components," she answered as she ducked into yet another shop. "After the confrontation with Zavala and her Coven friends, I decided I needed to stock up on a bit more than I already had on hand. If I'm going to defend myself, I will need a little more than just the bare essentials I've been carrying." Just as the other shops she had already investigated, there was nothing of value to her. Specifically, they had nothing that could be used as effective componentry for the spells she had available. Disappointed, she walked back out onto the sidewalk. "Unfortunately, there doesn't appear to be much of use here." The village was obviously not intended to be a magical resource, appearing instead to be nothing more than a quaint fishing village.

Mikel chuckled. "Had I known that was what you were looking for," he explained at Ahna's quizzical glance, "I would have been able to help sooner. You're right, there won't be a lot to be found here but we know of a much better place."

"You mean the dragon lady?" Vox asked with interest, looking up from the appetizing selection of smoked fish he had been perusing.

Mikel nodded. "Exactly."

"Dragon lady?" Ahna asked, apprehension evident in her voice. "Who is the dragon lady?" She wasn't entirely sure she wanted to know but the men didn't seem to be concerned. She, on the other hand, was more than a little worried. The last thing she needed at that very moment was to get involved in any way with a dragon, lady or otherwise.

"There's a keep not too far away from here where you should be able to find just about anything you need. It's called Dragon Keep. Vox and I helped out the owner a while ago. She's an alchemist so she spends almost all of her time either out hunting for components or in her lab manufacturing stuff. Because the keep is called Dragon Keep, she kind of inherited the nickname of dragon lady, but she's as human as any of us. Besides, you probably won't even encounter her, as the place is largely managed by a witch named Phemie."

Somewhat relieved by his explanation, Ahna calmed. However, his explanation had raised more questions. "By witch, do you mean real witch, or just a person who practices magic?" Ahna understood the difference between a mage such as herself and a witch. Although some people used the terms interchangeably, they were actually two very different things. Mages were formally trained and spent a lot of time learning how to grow and cultivate their magical abilities, which were supplemented with components and other items to gain larger effects from their spells. Witches, on the other hand, were born with much stronger natural abilities and were able to do things without having to be taught, either through inherent understanding of the magical fields or through their own power source.

Although witches could use components, should they so desire, the vast majority of the time they didn't need to use them. The most powerful and dangerous witches, Ahna understood, were those who had received magical training to enhance their own natural abilities. She wasn't certain, but she suspected that a witch such as that might even prove to be more dangerous than an actual dragon.

"She's a witch, all right," Vox assured her. "Even looks like one. Flies around the shop on an armchair, the funniest thing you'll ever see." He handed the shopkeeper a handful of coins in return for one of the smoked meats he had been drooling over moments before. "The smoked fish doesn't get any better than it is here," he said as he stuffed a piece into his mouth, offering more of the same to the rest of the small group. "Want to try some?"

"I asked her about that once, too," Mikel added as he accepted a sample of the offered fish. "She said she didn't have any formal training, so I guess that means she's a natural witch."

Ahna nodded slowly. She still wasn't too thrilled with the idea of dealing with a witch, not that she had any real reason to fear the woman. She simply couldn't be assured that the witch wasn't a part of the Grand Coven. From her own standpoint, she couldn't be too cautious. She had barely been strong enough to escape Zavala and her small pack; she couldn't imagine she would be able to take on a witch if Dragon Keep ended up being some sort of a trap as well.

Even worse, the name of the keep sounded familiar. She was fairly certain that Zavala had mentioned it to her at least once while they were still at the Academy. That fact gave her all the more reason to be suspicious. Realizing that Vox was offering his snack to her as well, she pulled a piece from the packaged meat and tasted it. It was warm and spicy, with a slight smoky flavor. "You were right," she admitted. "This is really tasty."

As though sensing the reason for her hesitation, Mikel put a reassuring hand on her shoulder. "They're good people," he said gently. "I wouldn't have suggested it if I thought there was any danger for you there."

Vox voiced his own opinions, similar to those

of Mikel, so Ahna agreed. "I just don't understand why they have been targeting me," she explained. "I know they said it was because my father was set to inherit the throne but with him dead, that means someone else will end up with it, not me."

"Maybe the witch will know something," Vox said. "Everyone at Dragon Keep is pretty well acquainted with the magical communities all over the place, so they might know something you haven't uncovered yet."

His idea had merit, so Ahna hitched her bag higher onto her shoulder, lifted her chin, and straightened her back. If her father had been able to see how much of a mess she had been these last few days, he would be appalled at the sight. A de Melville never showed weakness and she had shown nothing but weakness and hesitation since the previous morning.

While the incident with Zavala had taken her completely off-guard, she wasn't going to let something like that happen again. From now on, she vowed to both herself and to her ancestors, she was going to be the force with which they had to reckon. She was no longer a child, getting caught up in childish pursuits and waiting for someone else to come save her. No longer would she run and hide, no longer would she live in fear of what was to come. She was Countess de Melville, heir to one of the most powerful families in the Dracott Empire. If anyone thought they were going to get the upper hand on her, they would need a mighty tall ladder in order to achieve such a feat.

It was time to do something about it.

15

Their direction decided, the trio spent a short period of time deciding how to get to Dragon Keep. Their destination lay deep within the Inland Empire, almost to where Ahna had begun her journey in Three Rivers. In fact, Dragon Keep was further upstream of the Harrow River, one of the rivers that met to give the town of Three Rivers its name. The fact that Ahna had so strenuously objected to returning to the area near Three Rivers suggested that Zavala and her friends were unlikely to seek her there or anywhere in the vicinity of the Academy, Dragon Keep included.

"Staying on a ship would be my first choice," Vox said, "but there aren't any trading ships that go to Dragon Keep." The closest they could get by ship from Dive would be to Three Rivers and would have to find alternate transportation from there.

Ahna immediately vetoed the idea, having no desire whatsoever to set foot in Three Rivers so soon after Zavala's betrayal. While she rationally knew that Zavala's behavior and intentions were not indicative of every resident of Three Rivers and the Academy in which Ahna had spent so many years, she wasn't quite ready to place any faith in its remaining population. The very real possibility of more members of the Grand Coven being present in the town and academy gave her more than enough reason to avoid the area.

"We could take a caravan," Mikel suggested. "There are a handful that go in that direction, so overland it would take about a week, maybe a week and a half to get there."

"What about using the transport gate?" a woman in a long cloak interrupted the conversation. "Dive is on the gate network now, so you can get to wherever you want that's on the network using that. It's a lot cheaper than using a portal and definitely faster than a caravan." The upper half of the woman's face was covered and a long scar ran from beneath the hood down the side of her face.

"That could be an option," Ahna said, trying not to stare at the oddly-dressed woman, "but does Dragon Keep have one as well?"

"Last I checked it did," the mysterious woman replied. "Since that was only a few days ago, I assume the gate there is still intact."

While Vox and Mikel looked confused at the suggestion, Ahna knew precisely what the woman was talking about. "Phalant, a classmate of mine from the Academy, was working with a few of his friends to set up a network of inexpensive gates around the Inland Sea," she explained as they walked toward the center of town. "I'm not surprised that he has gotten the system up and running, as he was reasonably close to completing the research to develop a working prototype the last time I saw him." Technically, the last time she had seen Phalant was while he stood next to Magi Tanis after the dorm fire, a detail that didn't seem significant. In fact, before she had been cloistered away in so-called safety, she had heard discussion about the gate network among some of the other students and was surprised that they hadn't encountered one of the gates already.

"Are you sure?" Vox asked. "Sounds like this

might be another of those traps you've been concerned about."

"If I hadn't already known Phalant," she assured him, "I would be a lot more concerned. He's a very studious person so I would be surprised if he was involved in something as illicit as the Grand Coven."

"I don't want to be the naysayer here," Mikel pointed out, "but you trusted Zavala, too. Are you sure that you aren't mistaken about this Phalant fellow?"

"You have a good point," Ahna admitted, "but I still think that it's less risky to use one of these transport gates than to travel overland. I've heard plenty of horror stories about caravans traveling along the Inland Sea, there are simply too many bandits. In fact, I heard that the reason the Pirate Run got its name was because of the quantity of pirates who can be found there, attacking any merchant ship that comes along."

"True, usually ship travel is safer than overland travel because of brigands," Mikel said, "and there are a lot of pirates on the Run. Pretty much any ship that travels along the Run uses a team of guardians to defend the ship against attack, so there is definite danger there. Using the gate would get us to our destination a lot faster, I just worry that it's all just a little too simple."

"A targeted spell," Ahna explained, "could be placed into the gate, that's true. However, that would mean that every gate they've set up would have to have had the same enchantment in place when it was built and activated in order to ensure the target was caught in the trap, not to mention the chance that the target even uses the gate in the first place."

"Sounds like it wouldn't even be worth it," Vox said.

"Exactly."

Even better, in Ahna's opinion, was that the gate only cost a few silver sheckels for all three of them to travel, which was much more reasonable for transport costs than the tyro per person for using the portal. The line to use the gate was also nonexistent, a welcome change from the hours-long wait they had experienced elsewhere. The best part, in her opinion, was that traveling via the transport gate was much less disorienting than traveling by portal. Where the magic involved in the portal system was effective for long distances, it caused a substantial amount of dizziness, nausea, and vertigo to anyone who used it. The same symptoms were present with the gate system, just at a much lower intensity.

Dragon Keep was nothing like what she had expected, not that she had started out with many expectations. Her vision of a keep, even a small one, was a set of towering buildings rising majestically from the clifftops, perhaps a set of flags waving merrily in the breeze. While she hadn't traveled to many keeps during her lifetime before relocating to the Academy, she had been to a few and all of them fit that model. What she saw upon arrival, however, was a set of ancient, crumbling ruins that had long since seen the end of their days, with only a couple of buildings that appeared stable. A handful of shoppers and traders milled around, all of whom appeared every bit as underwhelmed as Ahna herself was.

"Are you sure this is the right place?" she wondered quietly. "This place hardly appears inhabited, let alone open for business."

"They're still renovating," Mikel explained. "Vox and I helped them put the storefront together about a year or so ago and it looks like they've got a tavern now, too."

"And an inn," Vox noted. "Definitely an improvement.

Still uncertain as to whether this place would prove as useful as the men had indicated but willing to accept their word for now, at least until she discovered otherwise, she followed them across the expanse of courtyard and into the closest building that appeared to be standing under its own power. There, she discovered plenty more shoppers, many more than the exterior had indicated would be inside. Despite the aged and worn exterior, the interior of the shop was clean, well-maintained, and positively brimming with goods for sale. A small chalkboard just inside the entrance advertised attraction philters for sale.

"Vox?" a voice called out over the din. "Is that you?" A petite woman with countless trinkets tangled in her hair came shuffling over to greet them. She wore a black dress that had been embroidered with dozens of sigils, protecting her against just about anything Ahna could imagine. It wasn't just her dress that was covered in sigils, she noted as the woman approached. Her body was even more covered in the protective tattoos than Ahna's own was. At least Ahna's sigils were constrained to her back. If this woman had any more glyphs placed, they would encroach onto her face.

"Phemie," Vox grinned as he hoisted the tiny woman into the air, circling her in a bear hug. "Boy, it's great to see you again."

"You two have been gone so long, I had begun to suspect we wouldn't see any more of you around these parts." Phemie grinned in return as Vox settled her on to the floor. "And you brought Mikel as well, how wonderful of you!"

When it was his turn, Mikel hugged her as well. After letting go, he introduced Ahna. "Not just us," he explained. "We brought a friend."

"I can see that, and a fine friend you brought for us as well." Phemie stepped closer to examine Ahna more closely. "From the Academy, I take it?"

"I..." Ahna stammered, "I was. But I'm not there anymore." She understood in an instant what Vox had meant when he said Phemie looked like a witch. If Ahna herself had to describe what a typical witch would look like, she would describe something rather similar to the woman standing before her.

"I can see that," the witch said as she hugged Ahna as well. "But any friend of these two is a friend of ours as well. We're always happy to meet new people, particularly magical practitioners such as yourself."

Ahna wasn't surprised at the woman's deduction that she was a mage. Even the barest amount of magical training showed how to determine the level of magical power a person possessed and, since Phemie was a witch instead of a trained mage, she probably just passively noted it in everyone she met. No wonder the shop specialized in magical componentry. The ability to see at a glance what had magical properties and what did not would make collection a breeze.

"Ahna needs supplies," Mikel said. "She's running a bit low on components and we didn't know of a better shopping place for components this side of Sapphire."

"Sapphire?" the witch snorted in derision and swatted his arm affectionately. "We've better stuff than even that overpriced metropolis can hope for. We're on the gate network now, so Wendi has been spending all of her time scouting all over the empire, looking for new and exotic goods for us to carry. I think you'll be pleased with the amount of componentry we carry now; it's even better than it was the last time you boys were here."

"I heard you even got a contract with Mc-Clannahan Trading," Mikel added. "I remember you mentioning something last time we were here about that being one of the things you guys would like to see as the business grew."

"Indeed, we did." Taking each of the men by an arm, Phemie led them off to the tavern, a connected building to the side of the trading center. She settled them at a table and took a seat to join them. "Plenty of time for shopping later," she explained to Ahna's quizzical look, "unless you are in too much of a hurry for a meal and a few minutes of socializing."

"Not at all," Ahna said, happy to have an excuse to sit and think for a few moments while the rest of the group caught up with their friend. So many things had been happening in such quick succession that she had barely enough time to breathe, let alone to come up with any sort of a real plan of action. "I think that a rest and a meal sound wonderful."

"Wendi isn't here right now, of course," Phemie

explained. "As I said, she's been out on the network scouting for more business. Either that or she's been down in her lab, coming up with new concoctions to sell. She's an alchemist," she explained to Ahna, "makes most of the specialty items we sell here.

"All of you are welcome to stay as long as you like, of course. The inn finally opened a short time ago, so there's plenty of room. After everything you boys did for us the last time you were here, your rooms are on the house. While you're here, you should try the snakewine, everyone loves it." She signaled for a bottle.

A man, tall enough to tower over even the tallest man Ahna had seen previously, carried a bottle over to their table and looked longingly at it as Phemie uncorked it. He stayed there until Phemie shooed him away.

"Snakewine?" Ahna asked doubtfully. She had heard of some strange beverages over the years but she had never heard of anything like that.

"It's made with distilled cobra venom," Phemie explained as she poured a small amount of amber liquid into each of their glasses. "Does wonders for virility, if you know what I mean." She followed the statement with a daring wink at the men. "People started to discover this stuff and it became an overnight sensation. Could barely keep enough in stock to keep everyone happy."

16

While the men and their boisterous friend caught up, Ahna took the time to reflect. She wasn't sure that she enjoyed the snakewine, passing her glass to Vox after only a sip. While she immediately understood why the drink was popular with men, as anything to increase their virility was likely to draw a crowd, the flavor was not to her liking. She preferred a lighter, sweeter wine over the sharp tang of the brew. Thankfully the tavern also kept a stock of snowberry wine, one of her personal favorites. She gratefully accepted the offered bottle and retreated to the room of the inn that Phemie had offered them, leaving the men to visit with their witch friend. She could use a little privacy for her thought process.

She sipped at the pale blue wine slowly as

she tried to remember everything her father had taught her about getting out of sticky situations. There was no doubt that the situation in which she currently found herself was the stickiest by far of all situations she had found herself in previously. *Slow down,* his calming, reassuring voice echoed in her head, *and take stock of what you know.*

She knew that her father, at the very least, had been killed. That fact had become painfully obvious, starting with the words of Magi Andress while she had been staying at the Academy and further evidenced by the whispered stories at every town to which they had traveled. "But what about my mother and brother?" she wondered aloud as she paced the breadth of the room. "I still haven't heard anything about them. They were probably killed at the same time as my father but I don't know that for certain yet." Her brow creased as she considered the possibility that they could yet be alive.

"For that matter, I've been operating under the idea that they were all killed by the Dark Star." She paused at the low table near the door and poured more wine into her glass. "But do I actually know that for certain? Rumors said that he killed them but rumors aren't always true. Wyrm said that he didn't kill them, that he wasn't anywhere near the Dracott Empire when he was killed." She paused again. "But how could he know that? How could Wyrm know for such certainty that the Dark Star wasn't in the Dracott Empire when it happened?" The only solution she could think of was that Wyrm somehow knew the identity of the assassin. When she had asked him about that possibility, he hadn't actually denied it.

"He knows," she whispered to herself. "He knows who the Dark Star truly is." But could she trust the loremaster? Not only his knowledge of the infamous assassin's identity, but also his statement that he had not been responsible?

That knowledge did little to help her at that moment, so she continued examining what she knew so far. "Zavvie and the others said something about them ordering my parents' deaths, so maybe the Grand Coven was behind it after all." That also indicated that her mother and brother were dead as well, further evidence that her original assumption about being the last member of her family remaining alive had been correct. "They could have hired the Dark Star, but Wyrm said he wasn't responsible. So why does everyone think it was the Dark Star who did it?" She pondered further, realizing that, as with all rumors, the idea of the Dark Star's responsibility for the deaths of the de Melville family had to have a point of origin, one that likely resided within members of the Grand Coven itself.

"But why would anyone want to frame an assassin?" That sounded like the worst possible idea in her mind, as setting up an assassin could only put a target on one's back. Particularly when the bounty on his head had become as high as it had. If she had been in the Dark Star's position, she would want to know who was responsible, that was for certain.

"Makes sense if you think about it," a familiar voice spoke up from the doorway. Mikel stood there, leaning against the door frame, arms folded across his chest, warhammer hanging at his side. "If I needed to frame someone for murder, particularly a person in a position of power like your father, an assassin, particularly a rather famous assassin who was known for feats of impossibility, would be a pretty good option. Nobody would even suspect that it was a frame-up and he can't exactly come forward and tell the authorities that he wasn't responsible, can he?"

"That makes sense. If he didn't kill my family, then there wouldn't be any reason for him to try killing me as well," she reasoned as she stepped closer to refill her wineglass again. "That means he probably wasn't the source of the fire in Sapphire."

"Probably not."

"Or the fire at the Academy." Beginning to fully realize that so many things were not quite as she had assumed them to be, she drained the glass and poured another, ignoring the raised eyebrow coming from Mikel. "After my father was killed, I was put into a protected location within the Academy, supposedly for my own safety in case whoever killed him came after me as well." She peered around the cleric but the hallway beyond him was empty. "Where's Vox?"

"He wanted some alone time to catch up with Phemie more privately so I left them to their vices. I thought you had said you were under a different name, an alias, while you were there," Mikel said. "How did they know to put you into protection after your father's death?"

"A few people knew the truth of who I was.

It was supposed to be a secret from everyone else but somehow other people found out." She took another drink, this one much smaller than the previous. "About a week before everything happened, Zavala came to find me and asked me if I was really a de Melville. Apparently, she had heard a rumor." She stopped pacing and turned to face him. "At least, that was what she said. But maybe she was lying." She really needed to reconsider how much faith she was to put into anything Zavala had ever told her. Her mouth began to twist into a scowl before she could help herself.

"Given everything we've seen, I doubt it was much of a rumor," Mikel pointed out. "From what happened in Aquos, I suspect she targeted you from the beginning."

"Yes. She had mentioned something to that effect also." Ahna refused to meet his eyes. Zavala's betrayal still hurt, far more deeply than she had expected. "She told me that she knew who I was the first time we met, and that she befriended me because of it." It stung badly, knowing that the person she had grown the closest to, the person she had trusted the most over the last three years, had been lying since the day they met. "How could someone be so cruel?" She hadn't intended to vo-calize the last of her thoughts but it whispered out regardless of her intentions.

"So maybe that means that the knowledge of your true identity wasn't as widespread as you had initially thought."

"Perhaps. I still don't know how members of the Grand Coven knew I had been moved to Three Rivers, or how she managed to find out where I was being hidden after the fire. I should have been safe there. Until I know more about both of those things, I can't risk going anywhere near the Academy or letting my guard down."

Mikel sighed and stepped into the room, set-tling down in a chair across from Ahna. "I may not know everything that happened between you and Zavala," he explained, "but I want you to know how sorry I am for not being there to protect you when you needed me."

"You don't need to feel badly about that," she reassured him. "She fooled all of us. I knew her for years and never suspected a thing. There was no reason for you to believe I was in danger while I was with her." She turned away, not wanting him to see the tears welling up in her eyes. She swallowed hard, willing the emotions to settle. Despite the brave face she showed to the rest of the world, Zavala's betrayal had cut deeply and would continue to fester for some time to come. She couldn't simply turn off the feelings she had once felt toward the girl any more than she could will the sun to stop shining in the sky. "If anything, I should be apologizing to you."

"To me? Why?"

"You saw that there was something wrong. You were the only one who even hinted that there might be something amiss in the whole situation. If I had only listened, perhaps things wouldn't have gotten so out of hand."

It looked like Mikel wanted to say something else but Ahna waved him away. "I think that what we all need right now is a good night's sleep. In the morning, we can figure out what to do next and where to go from here."

Understanding that she was done talking on the subject, Mikel left her in peace.

There were a handful of other people staying at the inn besides Ahna, Mikel, and Vox. Most of the other guests were only there for a single night to rest after a busy day of travel and shopping but others stayed for longer. The second day that they were at Dragon Keep, Ahna discovered that the goods in the storefront and the snakewine in the inn weren't the only draws to the keep. Behind the main building, an assortment of dangerous animals was on display, captured from all over the Inland Empire. There were a pair of gargoyles, a small handful of Ingnis lizards, a single chupacabra, and even a small squirm of cobras. "That must be how they are able to maintain their supply of snakewine," Ahna mused, remembering Phemie's explanation that the spicy wine had been made with cobra venom. "Brilliant."

She had seen some fine menageries back home in Ruschlack but none had been as impressive as the one at Dragon Keep. Most she had known had housed only animals common to the area and she wasn't sure she wanted to know how the people of Dragon Keep had gotten their hands on a chupacabra, let alone the pair of gargoyles. She spotted a pair of men that she recognized from her years of study in the Three Rivers Academy library, loremasters who were intently focused on the gargoyles. Unwilling to bring their attention to her, she slowly and quietly crept away. The last thing she needed at that moment, she was sure, was for the men to notice her and report her location back to the Magi at the Academy.

"Checking out the menagerie?" a voice interrupted her thoughts. Phemie glided silently alongside her, riding an overstuffed green armchair that had seen better days. "Come with me, we have some things to discuss."

Skeptical but curious, Ahna followed her.

"Vox told me that you're concerned about the Grand Coven," Phemie said once they were safely tucked into one of the back rooms of the store. "Don't worry," she raised a calm hand to Ahna's alarmed expression, "your secrets are safe here. Nobody needs to know anything about you that you don't want them to know.

"We deal with a lot of mages from the Academy at Three Rivers," Phemie explained, "primarily due to the proximity of the Keep to the Academy but also because I have cultivated relationships with many of the students and faculty over the years we've been in business here. I understand your concern about your safety at the Academy and I wanted to reassure you that it is completely warranted."

Ahna sat back in her seat, almost dropping the offered glass in surprise at the witch's words. What did she mean that it was completely warranted? Did the witch know something about Ahna's situation? "What are you trying to say?"

"I'm talking about the Grand Coven. Secret group of witches and mages who are scattered all over the country, taking over every empire they can get their claws into. Same group of people who have had you running for your life ever since you first stepped foot outside of the Academy, and even before that if the rumors I have been hearing hold any truth whatsoever." She leaned forward, her eyes darkening in sincerity. "You're in danger, girl."

"I know that." Ahna cast her eyes downwards. She had known the danger she and her friends were in from the beginning but having someone explain it so bluntly was unexpected, particularly when that somebody was a person that she had only met the previous day. "That's actually why we're here, to try and regroup, to get some breath-ing room, so we can figure out what our next steps are."

"So long as those next steps don't take you

anywhere near the Academy, you should be safe. For as long as you stay here, we will do everything under our control to ensure your safety."

Ahna set the glass down on a shelf, no longer trusting her own hands to hold it. She had no idea why, but she felt like she could trust the woman, witch or not. Perhaps it was because Mikel and Vox obviously trusted her, or perhaps it was because she badly needed a female friend in whom she could confide. Perhaps, the darker part of her soul realized, it was because she was simply too trusting, too willing to believe in the base honesty of other people. "I don't know what to do," she explained finally. "I've been wracking my brain, trying to come up with some way out of this but I've come up against one dead end after another. The people I thought I could trust have become the people betraying me the most, so I no longer know in whom I can place my faith. I don't know what to believe and what is just rumor. I just don't know where to go anymore."

As though she recognized the younger girl's discomfort, Phemie smiled reassuringly and patted her on the hand. "You're perfectly safe here, we don't put up with any of that nonsense in our keep. Crucian and Jaegar are pretty good at keeping the nonsense at bay. So you can stop worrying so much about the danger you might be in while you're here.

"Next, let's talk about your time at the Academy. I have reason to believe that a lot of the Magi and other faculty are secretly members of the Grand Coven. Not all of them, mind you, but enough to be more than just a nuisance. I suspect that at least some of them have been trying to get closer to you in order to recruit you into their group."

Ahna nodded. "My... well, I guess she's not exactly my friend anymore. She told me that they wanted me because of my family's connection to the Dracott Empire and Emperor du Toit in particular." She considered adding who she and her family connections were but wasn't sure she was ready to trust the witch with that much information yet. The more cautious part of her mind kicked her for even disclosing as much as she had, but she quickly shushed it down. Whether or not it was a bad idea, it was too late to go back and change it. Words could never be un-said, after all.

Phemie nodded. "That's probably one reason, sure, but there is another, equally important, reason I'd suspect was the real reason they were targeting you."

"Why would that be?"

"Because of your sheer magical power, of course. After all, the only thing worse than someone with your amount of magical power is someone with your magical power who is also in a position of political power. There was no way they could let that one go."

"But I'm not all that powerful," Ahna protested. "I mean, sure, I have some skills but I'm really not that strong."

"Sure you are," Phemie said gently. "In fact, I am absolutely certain that even if you had received no magical training whatsoever, you would still have posed a substantial threat to them." She sat back and smiled. "Trust me, it takes a witch to recognize a fellow witch."

The ground fell out from below Ahna and the periphery of her vision turned white as the words echoed in her head. A witch? Her? She shook her head slowly in denial. Even as she tried to dispute her words, however, a part deep inside her knew that there was some grain of truth to the witch's words.

"Furthermore," Phemie continued, "that very reason may have been a part in what brought you to the Three Rivers Academy to begin with. I know that there are plenty of places in the Dracott Empire to train prospective students in the magical arts but the Academy out here is simply better capable of handling people with natural talents such as yours."

The witch refilled the glass with cool, clear water and pressed it into Ahna's shaking hands. "Here, drink this. I'll give you a moment to process everything."

"Thank you," Ahna said finally. "But... even if everything you said is true – and I'm not disputing it's true, I'm just looking at all of the possibilities - that still doesn't get me any closer to figuring out how to get out of this mess."

Phemie waited for her to finish the water before speaking. "I think I may have a suggestion on that as well. I believe that I know the location of a member of the Grand Coven, one who has been absent from public view for a great many years. Well," she paused, examining her own fingers thoughtfully, "I really don't know whether she would be considered a current or former member, given how long she has been gone. But I suppose that doesn't really matter much at this moment.

"The point is, given the abilities possessed by both yourself and Mikel, I believe that we may be able to undo a curse that has blocked this particular Coven member's powers."

"Blocked her powers?" Ahna asked in confusion. "I don't understand. Why would Mikel and I want to lift this curse from a member of the Grand Coven? How are we supposed to help with something like that? How does one even get their powers locked away in the first place? Even more, wouldn't that just bring even more danger on all of us?" She definitely didn't think that removing some magical curse from a member of the group that had been hunting her, apparently for years, was a good idea. Further, she wasn't sure why Phemie would even suggest such an idea to her. Was the witch less of an ally than she had originally believed after all? Had Ahna made yet another mistake, the latest in a long line of blunders and errors of judgement that she had been making lately? Her mind whirled with possibilities, none of them good.

With a dismissive wave, Phemie said, "Don't

worry about the danger, there's no additional danger to any of you with this plan than there would be if you did nothing. There's no reason to fear this person, either. She is every bit as trustworthy as either of those men you have been traveling with." She blinked at Ahna closely before adding, "At least, I hope you've learned that they can be trusted by now. If not, we've got a whole host of other issues that we need to address with you."

"No, I know that they can be trusted." Ahna's voice was strained but her words were true.

"And there are a few other pieces that would need to fall into place before you would be able to do anything about this problem anyway."

"What kind of piece are you waiting for?" One thing that Ahna had quickly realized was that having a member of the Grand Coven, even a previous one, on her side seemed like it could be a very beneficial arrangement, assuming that the person in question was as trustworthy as Phemie had said. She still held some doubts close to her chest but she understood that a leap of faith was needed every now and again. It seemed, the time to make another leap had arrived.

"The mage in question had all of her powers

locked away in a trapping stone. The stone containing all of her powers is currently in possession of the Pirate King."

Ahna was horrified at the idea of a trapping stone. She had heard of them, of course, as had many of the other students at the Academy. Trapping stones were cursed items, capable of stealing the entirety of a mage's power. Angry as she was about what the Grand Coven had done, both to herself and to her family, the idea of actually using one of the horrid devices on anyone, no matter how evil, offended her to her core. Anyone who would resort to actually using one must have been equal parts cruel and desperate indeed. "So how do we get this stone?"

"As I said, its currently with the Pirate King. As you may guess, he isn't likely to just hand it over. I don't know where the Pirate King is," Phemie admitted, "but I think I may just know of someone who can help with that part.

17

Only a few hours after the next sunrise, Phemie came to gather Ahna, Vox and Mikel. She led them to the inn's meeting room, which had been closed off against the rest of the guests. "All will be explained shortly," the witch promised as she escorted them inside. "Just wait here and relax. Have some coffee or perhaps tea while you wait." She indicated a buffet against the rear wall, upon which rested an assortment of cups, saucers, bowls of cream and sugar, and a pair of steaming pots.

Next to arrive was a tall red-haired man who didn't so much walk into the room as swagger. His clothes were rough and work-ready but he carried himself with an air that was far above the working class. It was posturing with which Ahna was far too familiar, indicative of lower nobility at best. Many first-year students at the Academy had a similar walk, evidence of their family's financial status. Even back home that type of walk had indicated trouble, so she wasn't sure how much to expect seeing it now.

At the man's side walked a woman dressed in a floor-length grey cloak complete with a hood that had been positioned to cover most of her face. Her head rose to just over her companion's shoulder, her stride less arrogant but steady with purpose. A deep scar ran down the left side of her jawline, continuing further onto her neck.

"I know you," Ahna pointed out in surprise. "You're the woman who suggested we use the gate."

"Doesn't surprise me," the man chuckled. "She's been running all over the empire, trying to build up traffic heading in this direction. I'm Sean Mc-Clannahan and this is…"

The cloaked woman interrupted him. "This is someone capable of introducing herself," she glared at Sean. "Why do you always do that?"

"Because it makes you angry," he said with a saucy grin. "And then you get all mad, and then things get really interesting."

Somehow managing to glare at him through the hood, she turned back to the trio. "My name is Wendi," she said simply, ignoring the last set of remarks. "Feel free to ignore this idiot."

"Wendi?" Mikel asked, his voice incredulous. "You're Wendi? The owner here?"

"Wait," Vox said, apparently confused. "You don't look anything like a dragon."

Wendi chuckled. "I'm no more a dragon than you are. Lots of people call me the dragon lady because I own Dragon Keep. But the place had the name long before I came here. I just inherited it when I bought the place."

"Oh good," Phemie bustled back into the room only a few moments later. "You're all playing nice. I was a little worried." Behind her came another pair of people. The first was a small girl with dark brown hair and an eyepatch over her left eye, a pair of lethally hooked swords at her hips. A slender young man with a shock of bright red hair that was even more vibrant than Sean's and a scattering of freckles across his cheeks strode confidently alongside her.

The girl eyed Ahna and her group with

undisguised suspicion but the boy strode immediately over to Sean and punched him in the arm.

"What was that for?" Although the blow had obviously not been intended to harm, Sean rubbed the impact point anyway.

"That was for missing Uncle John's birthday," the boy explained.

"Okay everyone, let's play nice," Phemie interrupted before Sean had a chance to respond. "I know it's a bit early for some of you and a bit too public for others but we have a lot to discuss, so let's get to it, shall we?

"Let's start with introductions first. I know," she raised a hand at the murmurs that began arising from the gathered crowd at her statement, "most of you already know each other. Be that as it may, for those of you who are new, let's just all start out on an even playing field. As you all know, my name is Phemie, and I am a witch. This," she stepped next to Mikel and placed a hand on his shoulder, "is Mikel. He's a cleric of Pulia'a and a quite capable healer. Next to him is Vox, one of the best scouts I've seen in a long time." Muted greetings from the group followed each introduction.

"This," she placed a gentle hand on Ahna's

shoulder as she continued, "is Ahna de Melville, also a witch, formerly a student at Three Rivers Academy, and the eldest child of Count de Melville, the man who was in place to be the next emperor of the Dracott Empire. She is being targeted by the Grand Coven for both her family connections and her magical powers. At least three attempts have already been made on her life."

As the witch spoke, Ahna's eyes widened in shock and alarm. Quivering started in the pit of her stomach and quickly spread throughout her extremities at the witch's words. How did the witch know all that? She hadn't told anyone about her true identity in quite some while and her disguise, while imperfect, should have kept the suspicions at bay for a while longer yet. Worse, why had she announced it so clearly in front of a room that was filled with strangers?

Mikel's large hand clasped over her smaller one, reassurance that she was safe regardless of the information that was being shared. His presence, while reassuring, did little to calm her swiftly-growing fears. "What are you doing?" she hissed at Phemie. "You can't just announce things like that!"

"Don't worry, darling," Phemie responded with

a smile. "Everyone has secrets. Yours aren't even the worst of them." The witch turned her attention to the latest arrivals. "Some of you already know Keagan McClannahan, of the infamous McClannahans. You may even know Jasika," her hand hovered over the girl's shoulder but one unabashedly murderous glance kept her from making direct contact. "Of course, that's not her real name but it will suffice for today. Most of you probably know her better as the Dark Star, infamous assassin of the Dracott Empire."

Shocked silence fell across the room at her words and the girl introduced as Jasika shot to her feet, a dagger magically appearing in her hand as she spun on the witch. "What are you trying to do here?" Jasika demanded. Keagan placed a calming hand on her arm in an attempt to get her to lower her dagger.

This was the infamous assassin known as the Dark Star, the terror of the Barberry Empire? The girl hardly looked old enough to travel on her own. Despite that, her lightning-fast movements and the telltale swords on her hips attested to the truth. Ahna didn't understand what could cause such a little girl to become an assassin, nor what could drive her to the success she had earned. *How young must she have been,* she mused, *to have amassed a reputation such as the one for which she was known?*

"As I said," Phemie responded calmly, without the slightest hint of fear in either her voice or her posture, "I'm making introductions." She stepped to the next person in the group. "Sean McClannahan, obviously also a McClannahan, cousin to Keagan as well as son of the mayor of Hoem."

Well, Ahna thought, *that certainly explained the swagger.*

"Last but certainly not least, we have Wendi, also not her real name but close enough for daily use. She is the owner of this keep and a former member of the Grand Coven, the same group that has been targeting Ahna."

With resigned motions, obviously used to such antics from the wildly-dressed witch, Wendi raised her hands as Phemie spoke, pushing the hood away from her face until it fell against her back. When she raised her head to look squarely at the rest of the group, Ahna couldn't hold back a cry of alarm.

The woman had no soul. She was a demon, certainly.

Her heart thundered in her chest as she remembered Phemie's words about a former member of the Coven, the person whose powers had been stolen, powers to whom she wanted Ahna to restore. This demonic creature had to be the person to whom she was referring but how could she restore the powers of a necromancer? Particularly when that necromancer was a member of the group who wanted her dead? The air itself seemed to thicken and close in around Ahna's head and she found it difficult to breathe. Her chest, already tightened by the first portion of introductions, now felt as though it was encased in a corset that had been laced too tightly.

"Please excuse me," she staggered toward the door, manners somehow equally balancing fear even in her heightened emotional state. "I need some air."

Mikel and Vox joined her but thankfully the rest of the group remained inside. "I can't do this," she explained, her voice shaking. "She's a necromancer." She needed to get herself back under control, otherwise she was going to faint from lack of breath. A handful of travelers, arriving at Dragon Keep for a day of shopping and exploration, looked at the trio curiously but made no move to approach.

"You don't have to do anything," Mikel stressed, hand clasping her shoulder for both physical and mental support and stability. "If you want to leave, we can leave right now."

Vox nodded his agreement. "But it might be worth hearing what they have to say," he pointed out. "More information, regardless of what you decide to do with it, is always better."

Ahna looked between the men, willing her breathing to calm and her knees to continue holding her off the ground. Her mind was swimming but she realized that, despite everything that had just been revealed, nobody had appeared ready to attack. Except Jasika, she supposed. The woman had appeared ready to kill Phemie for her announcement. Despite appearances, however, she hadn't actually attacked, possibly because of Keagan's interference.

Was that really the infamous assassin of whom Ahna had been so afraid? She had never even suspected that the Dark Star could be a woman, it was generally assumed to have been a man. After a few long moments of slow, deliberate breathing, she felt better in control of herself.

"The Dark Star," she said finally. "Can that little girl really be the Dark Star? I never would have suspected. She's so young!" She looked from Vox to Mikel and then towards the meeting room they had just left. "And the necromancer, member of the Grand Coven. They really are everywhere. How could I have not known?"

"Why would you have known?" Mikel asked gently. "Assassins thrive on misinformation and staying hidden. The fact that most people don't expect a woman to attack them actually makes a lot of sense when you think of it that way. People are on guard against attack from men but nobody suspects a woman to be the danger. Look at your own history, for example. You never thought that Zavala would cause problems for you but she turned out to be the biggest threat."

Ahna nodded slowly. "But the necromancer. Phemie wants us to restore her power, how can I do that?" Her mind flew back in time, to the attack on Tomens. Could that have been the same necromancer whose powers she had now been tasked with restoring? Was the scarred woman inside the meeting room, the woman whose eyes held no soul, the person responsible for all those deaths? It had been so long ago, Ahna couldn't quite re-call how many had fallen in the attack, only to be raised to fight once more, this time against their very brethren. She shuddered, less at the memory but more at the idea of what could happen if she restored the woman's powers. Assuming she had been responsible for the previous attack, would she do it again?

On the other hand, she had to consider that if Phemie had been telling the truth, if the people in-side the small meeting room were as trustworthy as she had indicated, she couldn't ask for a better set of allies. The most infamous assassin, the great-est threat to the lives of everyone she had ever known. A necromancer, member of the secretive Grand Coven. If she had two people such as that on her side, she may just find a way to survive the ordeal. If absolutely nothing else, the two women she had just met could be a valuable resource, a source of information that had been unavailable to her until now.

"You don't have to do anything," Mikel

reminded her. "Whatever you decide to do, Vox and I will back you completely." Vox nodded his agreement and Ahna made up her mind.

"I'm tired of running," she said, her voice far more assured of her decision than she really felt. "I'll hear them out, find out what they expect to happen, and then I'll decide what to do. But for now, you're right, Vox. I need to know as much as I can and there's no better place for me to find out what's really going on right now."

Without another word, she straightened her spine and strode into the meeting room.

"Jasika is going to go after the Pirate King," Phemie explained once the trio took their seats once more. "He has the trapping stone, the one I mentioned to you a while ago, and she has an idea of where he can be located. Once we have that back, assuming you're still willing to try, we can work on restoring Wendi's power."

"Pirate King?" Ahna looked at the witch, trying to figure out how pirates could possibly fit into the current situation. Had something else happened while she had been outside? "What is the Pirate King doing with the trapping stone?" She wasn't sure she wanted to know how Jasika knew how to find him but if the girl truly was who Phemie said she was, she would undoubtedly have some means by which to do so.

"Before I came here, before he was the Pirate King, he was my guild leader," Jasika explained. "He was the one who sent me to take away Wendi's powers after she finished her assignment."

Ahna looked from the witch to the assassin, not sure she had understood correctly. "You were the one who took her powers?" When Jasika nodded, she asked, "so why do you need Mikel and I to restore them? If you knew how to take the magic in the first place, then you should know how to restore it, too." Her previous suspicions that the Dark Star may somehow have magic at his back resurfaced.

Jasika shook her head. "I barely knew how to use the thing. I was just given minimal instructions on its use and that was it. Had I known what I was doing, I probably wouldn't have done quite so much damage to Wendi in the first place."

"Damage?" Ahna turned from Jasika to Wendi. "What kind of damage?"

"The scar, for one," Wendi supplied, gesturing to the jagged mark that crossed her face. "For the longest time, I thought that the black eyes were a part of the same thing but it was only recently I discovered what had caused those. But the biggest thing is my memories."

Ahna blinked at her, wondering what her memories had to do with anything. "What memories?"

"Exactly. I have none."

Ahna blinked at her again but then her eyes widened in comprehension. "You did it wrong," she whispered to nobody in particular.

"Yes," Jasika answered simply. "After quite a bit of consideration, we're pretty sure she wasn't supposed to survive it."

"That's why you needed me," she turned her attention to Phemie. "Did you know I specialized in mental magic?"

Phemie nodded. "I have a friend who teaches at the academy, he had mentioned a gifted mental artist he met recently. It didn't take long to recognize that you were the person about whom he had spoken."

"Did you attack Tomens?" Ahna needed to know before she made any decisions so she turned her attention to the death mage. "About seven years ago, a necromancer assaulted Tomens, an entire army of the undead slaughtering their way through town. The city was devastated and those who fell in battle were brought back to life to fight again, to fight against their own people, more soldiers in the undead army. Was that you? Did you do this horrible thing?"

"They weren't brought back to life," Wendi said. "Not if there was a necromancer involved. We don't restore life, that's not even a possibility with our magic. Life has never been ours to give, only to take."

Her admission, far more direct than Ahna had expected, still didn't answer the question. "Was it you?"

"I don't know," Wendi admitted. "I heard about it, sure, but all of that happened just before the first memories I have. I only remember back to a few months after that happened." She smiled ruefully, with no trace of humor behind her smile. "It probably was, though. Something that big could easily account for my eyes."

"Why?" Ahna needed to know. "Why attack Tomens? What could you possibly have gained from that?"

"I don't know," Wendi said sadly. "As I said, I don't remember any of it."

"The Horn of Ascension." Jasika interrupted before anything more could be said. "She was after the Horn."

Ahna knew exactly to what she was referring. The Horn of Ascension was legendary in her hometown, in all of the towns of the Dracott Empire. As next in line for the throne, her father was to have received the Horn upon the death of Emperor du Toit. Until that time, it was locked securely in the palace vault. "If that's true, then it was all for nothing," she said finally. "All those people dead, all that horrible fighting, it was all in vain. Even the most powerful of necromancers couldn't get through the palace defenses."

"Not true," Jasika pointed out. "She was successful."

"What do you mean, she was successful? The Horn is still in the palace."

"The Horn is in Hoem." Jasika said. "I've had it for the last few years."

"You... what?" There was no way that the assassin had been in control of the Horn of Ascension. Everyone knew that whoever possessed the

Horn was automatically entitled to the throne. Had she really been in possession of it, she could have taken the entire empire with no room for argument at any time. "But Emperor du Toit is still on the throne," she said. "That means he has the Horn."

"The theft was covered up," Jasika admitted, "but I assure you, the Horn is *not* in the Dracott Empire."

"Perhaps that was what Zavala had meant," Mikel offered. "You'd said earlier that she had a plan for putting you on the throne if you joined them."

Vox nodded. "If the Grand Coven got their hands on this Horn, all they'd have to do is put into someone's hands, someone who was loyal to them. That would put the Coven in charge of an entire empire."

"So why not just give it to another of their members, then? They couldn't have possibly just been waiting for me this whole time. Didn't they have a plan after stealing the Horn?"

"They probably did," Jasika answered, "but I stole it from Wendi before they got a chance to do anything with it."

"And without the Horn, they can't put anyone on the throne." With all of the new pieces of information she had learned so far that morning, Ahna no longer knew which was the most shocking. As she looked around the gathered group, she realized that she wasn't the only one who hadn't known anything. Every person, other than Phemie, had looked surprised at one piece of information or another. Somehow, Phemie's lack of surprise at everything was almost understandable.

No wonder the witch had gathered them all together.

"So what's the plan?" Ahna asked finally. "I assume you guys have one, if you are going after the trapping stone."

"That's just phase one," Phemie said. "We'll fill you in on the rest while they're gone."

18

Ahna, Vox, and Mikel remained at Dragon Keep for the next few weeks, waiting for word from Jasika. She spent the first day exploring the Keep, from the inn in which she and the men were staying to the tavern where Vox had discovered he liked snakewine to the shop where all manner of strange goods could be found. She was finally able to stock up on all of the components she could ever hope for, which had been her primary reason for coming to Dragon Keep in the first place. There, she discovered that even gargoyle horn and roc feathers were in stock, two of the components she had expected to have the most trouble finding.

"That's why we have the menagerie," Crucian explained. He and Jaegar, the tall fellow Ahna had met in the tavern during her first meeting with

Phemie, both worked at the Keep and were friends with Phemie and Wendi. According to Phemie, the four of them had spent years traveling across the empire, exploring the area before settling down at the keep and opening the shop. "Wendi still goes out hunting sometimes but it's easier to get when the stuff is in the backyard."

On the same afternoon Jasika and Keagan left, two more members of the McClannahan family arrived. Dane was tall, blond, and broad-shouldered, lacking the trademark red hair of his family. He was accompanied by a woman who Ahna had first believed to be his wife but had been corrected quickly. "This is Dominique," he introduced her. "She's my cousin."

Ahna recognized Dane, although it took a few minutes of talking with him and Dominique to discover from where she knew him. When he mentioned the Bullfrog, the trading ship that he had recently been given captainship of, she smiled. "I was recently a passenger of yours," she explained. "You brought us from Aquos to Dive."

Dominique had waves of dark auburn hair cascading around her shoulders, only showing the trademark red glints when the light shone directly upon her. She wore the clothes of a warrior, accessorized by a rapier in its scabbard attached to her belt. Ahna had always been fascinated by female warriors, strong capable women who defied all of the stereotypes of men-at-arms and refused to accept their place as being in the home. Unlike Jasika, who radiated an air of not wanting to talk with anyone about anything, Dominique was friendly and open, completely willing to share a bottle or two of snowberry wine with Ahna to discuss her various exploits.

"I can't believe you're a ship guardian," Ahna said, impressed. Very few women were skilled enough to work in such a position, yet another defiance of traditional gender roles. "That's a really dangerous job, especially out on the Pirate Run!"

"Yeah, it can be," Dominique admitted, "The first handful of times I was on the ship, I barely even knew what I was doing. I wasn't used to fighting on a moving surface like on the ship, particularly when we start tacking back and forth to keep from getting rammed. It got easier once I got my sea legs under me, so now I can move even better on a ship than I can on land. That doesn't stop the attackers from ganging up on me, though.

They always seem to think that just because I'm a woman, that means I'm going to be an easy target." She chuckled. "Even that got a whole lot easier when Jasika joined the team."

"She's a ship guardian too?" Ahna couldn't imagine what had brought a notorious assassin such as the Dark Star to the point where she needed to act as a ship guardian. "Aren't you afraid to work with someone like that?"

"We didn't know who she was, at least not at first. When she first came aboard, she was just another passenger. The first time we got attacked after she boarded, she was pretty adamant about defending her own stuff. We probably should have guessed there was something unusual about her then. She stood in one place – one place! – outside her bunkroom door and took out a whole pile of pirates on her own, didn't even get scratched. Second time, she fire-bombed the attacking ship, practically sank it before they even had a chance to board us. That's when Uncle John offered her a job with the guardians. Still, nobody even got suspicious until she boarded an attacking ship by herself and apprehended the captain for the bounty on his head. By the time we discovered who she really was, she had been a member of the crew for a while and we all trusted her."

Considering what she claimed to have been carrying around at the time, Ahna couldn't really blame Jasika for wanting to defend it. She couldn't even imagine what would have happened if the Horn of Ascension had fallen into the hands of the pirates who terrorized the Run. She still didn't understand why the girl hadn't used the Horn to take control of the Dracott Empire, but she assumed she had her reasons. Assuming, of course, that she truly had the Horn of Ascension in her possession, as she had claimed. Ahna still wasn't sure she believed that quite yet.

The idea of trusting an assassin to any degree at all sounded like a poor plan to Ahna but she had to admit if anyone was capable of defending the ship and the artifact she carried, it was the Dark Star. She also recognized that she was in no position to judge, as she was putting a lot of her own faith into the woman at the moment, assassin or not.

"Enough about Jasika," Dominique refilled their glasses. "I want to know more about you. How did you get tangled up in this whole mess?"

"That's a bit difficult to explain," Ahna said with

a halfhearted shrug. "I was just a normal student at the Academy for the last few years. I got caught up in everything when people started killing my family and trying to kill me, too." She explained about the fire at the Academy and her harrowing escape through a window, greatly aided by one of the Magi.

"I heard about your family," Dominique met her eyes, sympathy etched across her face. "I'm so sorry to bring that back up again. I can't imagine what I would do if something like that happened to my family."

"I'm sad about it, of course. Growing up like I did in a family like mine, the possibility of assassination is just something we expect, so it wasn't as much of a surprise as it might have been otherwise. We're constantly on the lookout for people trying to kill us." She sipped at her glass, eyes downcast. "But perhaps not as watchful as we should be."

"Sean told me about your friend," Dominique reached out to cover Ahna's hand with her own. "I think it's terrible that she manipulated you like that, particularly for so many years. I have no idea how anyone could pretend to be someone's friend for so long, it's simply awful! Just leaving home, being in a strange new empire far away from everything you knew, she took so much advantage of you, I'd like to have a word with her myself. Nobody deserves to be treated like that."

Others arrived at the Keep as well. The next to appear was a slender man with a pair of swords at his hips and no hair on his head, or anywhere else on his body, as far as Ahna could tell. A massive man with long hair tied back behind him and almost as much muscle as the average bear walked alongside the hairless man, a foil-wrapped tray in his hands. The newcomers went directly to Sean and Wendi, where the larger man offered the package to Wendi and the smaller man clasped wrists with Sean.

"Those are Oree and Hannibal," Dominique explained. "They've been best friends with Sean since they were all still in diapers." As she refilled both of their glasses, she explained that Oree's grandfather worked on the Temptress with Jasika and Keagan.

"That's Cookie's grandson?" Ahna asked, amazed. Cookie was so warm and friendly but Oree seemed much colder and more calculating. In reality, he reminded her a bit of Jasika, both in his social behaviors and his manner of walking. There was no question that he was a dangerous man. It seemed very strange for a cold boy such as Oree to have come from the lineage of a warm man such as Cookie.

"Hannibal's mom runs a bakery in town," Dominique added. "If you ever get a chance, you need to try her sticky buns. They're to die for. I'd bet those are what he brought for Wendi; she's been addicted to them since the first time he brought them for her." If the scent wafting towards them on the light breeze was any indication, Ahna could completely understand that kind of addiction. Hopefully one day she would be able to go visit Hoem, perhaps even with her newfound friend, and sample them for herself.

The next to arrive were a threesome that needed no introductions as far as Ahna was concerned. "Is that Phalant? What's he doing here?" Phalant was flanked by Remy and Analisse, two other mages that Ahna recognized from Three Rivers Academy. The three of them had been the team developing the new transport gate system, a relationship that obviously extended beyond the educational walls. "I didn't expect to see anyone from the Academy here."

"They're friends of Phemie and Wendi too."

"Oh." On the one hand, Ahna was becoming less and less surprised by the minute at how far Phemie's influence extended. She remembered that Phemie had mentioned, in an off-hand way, that she cultivated relationships with people from the Academy. Far from the low-key witch she appeared to be, the woman was well connected indeed. "Are you certain that we can trust them?" While she already knew she could trust Phalant, she knew almost nothing about his companions.

"Absolutely. There's no way any of them are involved in this mess. Phemie wouldn't have brought them here otherwise."

The last to arrive, and by far the biggest surprise to Ahna, was a Magi from the Academy, one with whom she was well familiar. "Magi Andress?"

"Ahna, so good to see you," Magi Andress headed straight toward her, eyes wide and arms outstretched in greeting. "And safe, no less. I was worried when you disappeared, thinking that the Grand Coven had gotten their hands on you after all."

"You knew?"

"Of course I knew." He lowered his voice before continuing. "Almost all of the instructors knew that the Grand Coven had a presence at the Academy. Some of us had been trying to find a way to oust them before they caught on to who you were."

"Your intentions didn't turn out very well," she said ruefully. "Zavala was one of them. She admitted as much to me quite explicitly when she tried to kill me. She knew precisely who I was from the very beginning."

"Zavala?" Magi Andress's eyebrows raised in surprise. "We had no idea."

"Nor did I."

When a week passed with no word from Jasika on the success of her mission, Ahna started to get worried. While she understood that the woman was highly trained and likely needed no assistance, she still experienced a mental disconnect when trying to align what she had seen of the small woman and the legends she had heard of the Dark Star. While they waited, she tried her best to be helpful around the keep, assisting Jaegar with restocking supplies in the shop and casting a minor spell to tidy up the guest rooms at the inn as they were vacated by overnight guests. Most of her time, however, was spent in the company of Dominique, each enjoying the company of each other over a bottle or two of wine. Her fondness of the woman grew with each conversation, whether lengthy or otherwise, and Dominique appeared to feel the same. At least, Ahna assumed it was reciprocated, considering the number of times the swordswoman came to find her for yet another conversation.

A few times, she considered talking more with Wendi, still uncertain about her agreement to help the death mage. Rather than approaching her directly, she stayed back and observed. As far as she could tell, the woman was far more of an alchemist than a necromancer, spending the majority of her time either in her underground laboratory or quarreling with Sean. She wondered at the nature of their relationship, which appeared at times to be romantically close and at other times to be completely at odds with each other. Even when the pair was fighting, however, there was a strange undercurrent in the squabbles which Ahna didn't quite understand.

Others began expressing their concerns about Jasika and Keagan's extended absence when the second week passed with no word from them. "If I had a personal item of hers," Ahna offered during one of the many conversations about the wait, "I could try scrying for them to see if we need to send help."

"That could work," Oree said as he rose to his feet. "I know where her place is, so I can head there and be back before nightfall."

"No, wait." Both Vox and Hannibal, acting almost in unison, grabbed him before he took his first step. "There's no way she'd leave her home defenseless. It'll be heavily trapped."

"Why would a ship's guardian need to worry about trapping her house?"

"Why would a ship's guardian be sent out, alone, after the Pirate King?" Hannibal lowered his eyebrows at his friend. "Or do you think that maybe she's just a little bit more dangerous than just a guardian?"

Still not quite comprehending but apparently willing to trust his friend, Oree sat back down. "What should we do, then?" he asked. "I don't think any of us wants to just sit around here waiting for them to get back, there must be something we can do in the meantime."

"Defenses," Sean suggested. "If she's after the Pirate King, chances are pretty good that they'll be here again soon enough."

"Why would they know to come here?" Ahna asked.

"Because they've done it once before," Sean explained. "Last time, they were just after Wendi but this time they'll be a lot angrier."

Wendi, who had taken a respite from her laboratory to join the group, nodded her agreement. "And less likely to fall for the same trap as last time, too." She looked around the group and explained. "Pirates attacked the keep a few months ago. They wanted me and an item they thought I had. We managed to chase them away..."

"We?" Sean interrupted. "Pretty sure some of us played a larger role in that than others did."

"Yes," Wendi glared at him, "We. All you did was shoot one of them. Typical behavior for you, letting others do all the work and taking all the credit for yourself."

"Get a room, you two," Phemie interrupted the burgeoning argument. "But Sean does have a point. We should put some better defenses in place in case they do come back here again." She looked from Hannibal to Oree and then to Vox. "Do you guys think you can come up with something useful? You can use Jaegar and Crucian too. They're strong and between them they have most of a brain so they can follow basic instructions."

"You want me to help with that too?" Mikel asked.

"No," Phemie shook her head. "We need you to rest up and do whatever you need to do in order to get the curse lifted from Wendi as soon as Jasika and Keagan get back. That goes for you too," she included Ahna in her glance at the last comment.

It took almost an entire additional week, with most of the group toiling away at bolstering the defenses of Dragon Keep, before Keagan came stumbling through the transport gate, a bleeding and broken Jasika in his arms. "Mikel!" he shouted as soon as he was through the gate. "Mikel!"

Dropping the book he had been reading, Mikel rushed to the boy's side, warhammer at the ready. He lifted the girl out of Keagan's arms, rushing her back indoors to examine her wounds more closely.

She had neither of her trademark hooked

swords and her clothing was torn to shreds, revealing gaping wounds beneath the strips of cloth, some of which had cut through muscle and struck bone. Where her skin wasn't red with blood or purple with bruise, it was a pale white pallor, slightly ashen as though she was already more than halfway into death's realm. A dark red trail led from the girl to the gate through which she had been carried.

"I'll be fine," Jasika tried to wave him off. Her voice was far weaker than it should have been, barely above a whisper. She reached up with shaking hands and pulled a platinum chain from around her neck. At the base of the chain hung a black pendant in the shape of a skull. "Go work on Wendi. They'll be here soon."

"How are you even alive?" Mikel asked, amazed at the amount of damage she had taken. "Let me heal you up a little bit first."

"No time." Jasika struggled out of his arms, groaning in pain at the slight movement. "The pirates know I attacked them and they'll be here soon. They can't risk Wendi getting ahold of that pendant. You need to fix her and you need to do it now."

"I can take that," Ahna slipped the blood-stained trapping stone from the assassin's hands. "I've never worked with one of these, so I need at least a little bit of time to figure out how it works. In the meantime, let Mikel take care of your wounds."

She carried the necklace into the inn and settled herself in the meeting room. The need to examine the artifact had been expected, as she had known she would need to understand the underlying enchantments before she could release the trapped magic from the stone. The fact that the enchantment to trap Wendi's magic had been done incorrectly only added to the difficulty. Quietly, Analisse and Phalant joined her in her research, as did Magi Andress. Pages scattered across the table and writing implements quietly scratched notes across the pages.

After almost an hour of study, the group was joined by Remy. "Jasika had some information about the stone," he explained as he settled in among the group. "Since she was the last one to use it, she gave me the information she has on how it worked."

That information proved valuable, as with it

the group was able to decipher much more of what they were seeing. Before the next hour had passed, Ahna understood how the item worked and what she needed to do to release it.

"Are you certain about this?" Magi Andress pulled her aside as the group completed its task. "This is almost as dangerous of a casting as the initial trapping was. I'm not sure that I feel comfortable letting a student such as yourself attempt it."

Ahna had three separate responses to the Magi's warning. "First of all," she said, "I don't think I'm still considered a student. I may not have graduated but that doesn't matter very much right now. Secondly, I have more protections upon my person than anyone else here so I would be the most likely person to survive in case something goes wrong. And thirdly, in all due respect, that isn't your decision to make. It's mine."

"They're here," Jaegar called out to everyone. "But they don't look much like pirates."

Confused, Ahna peered through one of the windows that had a clear view of the courtyard. Billowing smoke flowed across the open area, slowly solidifying into human shapes. "It's the

Grand Coven," she said quietly. "That's the same thing they did in Aquos."

"There's no time left," Phemie pushed Wendi toward her. "If we're doing this, we need to do it now. You take care of her and I will head out to defend the keep. We'll give you as much time as we can but don't take too much of it!"

Magi Andress in tow, she scurried out the door and into the fray.

19

"Let's get this over with," Ahna said as she turned toward the hooded death mage. "Maybe once you have your magic back, you can lend some support to the people out there, hmm?" While she still had reservations about what she had agreed to do, she couldn't allow Jasika's sacrifice to have happened in vain. By restoring the necromancer's stolen magic, they all just might survive the day. She guided Wendi to recline on the sofa and settled down next to her. "This is probably going to hurt," she said apologetically.

"Don't worry about any sort of pain," Wendi said, her voice surprisingly soft and calm. "I can handle that. Just do whatever you need to do." She tilted her head back, folded her hands across her stomach, and closed her eyes.

The amount of trust that Wendi was placing in her was astounding, in Ahna's opinion. She wasn't sure she would be able to do the same, had their situations been reversed. However, she also knew that there was no way she could fully understand the other woman's situation or all that she had been through. Whatever she had done in her previous life, whoever she had been, all of that was gone. All that remained was the woman lying on the sofa before her. A woman who had just placed her life into Ahna's hands, the hands of a woman she had known for less than a month.

"And don't worry about me, either." Ahna directed the comment toward Mikel. "I know what Phemie said and I know you. I don't want you to turn your attention to anything other than Wendi until this is done."

"If something happens to you," Mikel tightened his hands on his warhammer as the sounds from outside grew louder, "there won't be anyone left to finish releasing her magic. That would mean this would all have been for nothing."

"I know," Ahna said as she gathered her components and arranged each of them within reach. "But I have a sigil on my back, one that will start to release healing magic if I start taking too much damage." She smiled mirthlessly at her friend. "When you're about to be the emperor of the Dracott Empire, you take extra precautions to ensure that your children cannot be used as leverage against you. I had a lot of safeguards put into place before being sent to Three Rivers to join the students of the Academy."

Along with the time she had spent getting to know Dominique and preparing for this day during Jasika's absence, Ahna had also spent a lot of time with Phemie. The witch had even more tattoos of protective sigils than Ahna herself possessed and had been able to identify and inform her about what the ones she hadn't yet identified had been. She had discovered that the air bubble that had saved her when Zavala and her cronies had attacked her in Aquos had been triggered by blood from that same attack, safeguarding her until she was able to reach a more secure area. The sigil upon which she was relying now, however, was the one that would trigger a regeneration spell as soon as she started receiving the damage she knew would erupt from the stone as soon as her spellcasting began.

Wendi wasn't the only one who was about to be in extreme pain. Ahna was certain that it had been that discovery that had caused Magi Andress to suggest he should spearhead Wendi's power return, the suggestion that Ahna had vetoed as soon as he said it. In order to release the trapped power, Ahna would feel the same amount of pain as Wendi herself did, as they would share the damage caused during the spellcasting.

"It's your friend," Vox called from the doorway where he had been stationed as a guard. "And she brought her friends with her, along with a few more."

"How many are out there?"

"Don't worry about it yet, Phemie's giving 'em hell. So are your mage friends."

As Ahna started casting her spells, she did her best to shut everything out of her mind. She didn't need to worry about how the battle in the courtyard was going, she had faith that her friends would do the best they could to ensure everyone's safety. She didn't need to know at that moment what she was going to do about her family or the discoveries she had made during her adventures. She didn't need to worry about the life that would lie ahead of her, should she survive this day. On that note, she didn't need to worry about whether or not she or any of her newfound friends would survive this day either, much as she hoped they all would. All she needed to worry about was untangling the magic that was trapped within the black skull medallion so that it could flow back into its rightful owner.

"Uh oh," she heard Vox mutter. "Looks like the pirates decided to come play after all."

"You go ahead," Mikel called over to him. "We'll be fine in here."

"Will do," Vox responded. "I'll do my best to keep them away from here while you guys are working, though."

The spell to release the trapped magic was simple, Ahna had to admit. By slowly and carefully reciting the incantation that she and the rest of the mages who had helped her research the item had worked out, she would be able to lead the stolen magic back to its owner in a steady trickle. That was one of the most dangerous aspects of the operation, as she understood full well the damage that could be caused by magical transfer that happened too swiftly. If that was to happen, the best scenario would be that the magic would escape completely and not return to its rightful owner, leaving Wendi in exactly the state she was currently in. The worst-case scenario was that all of the magic would flood into her at once, a lethal deluge of power that almost nobody could possibly survive.

Since they were sharing the damage, it was likely that Ahna would die as well. All she needed to do was to recite the spell slowly and carefully, making no mistakes as she did.

An arrow landing inches from her head startled her, distracting her as she spoke the last few words of the spell and causing her to gasp reflexively in surprise and she knew she had done it wrong. As though to punctuate that fact, the sigils on her back flared to life.

The talisman exploded, sending shards of glassy black material in every direction. The ball of energy, magic that Ahna had hoped to reintroduce gently into its host, slammed into Wendi with a tangible crash. She, in turn, levitated a few inches off of the cushion with the impact, shrieking in agony as the power flowed into and through her.

Skin began to peel away from Wendi's body, revealing muscle and bone beneath.

Mikel, continuing to pray even as the women screamed, held his warhammer, the symbol of his deity, over her as she floated further upwards until she collided with it. A secondary detonation of magical energy exploded through the room in a thunderous blast, shattering the glass from the windows. The cleric rapidly repaired the skin as it ripped away from Wendi's body, healing the damage almost as swiftly as it occurred. A puddle of blood began to gather on the floorboards beneath her, too much for the couch to readily absorb.

Ahna watched, unable to move, as Wendi's power swirled around and through her body. It trickled out through every lesion as it opened, stopping only when Mikel closed each wound up once more. Ahna, for her part, maintained barely enough focus to keep the swirling energy nearby, unwilling to lose any more of Wendi's magic than absolutely necessary. More than once, she felt herself fading from consciousness from the onslaught of magical damage and the resulting pain, only to feel her tattoos flare again and again, releasing their own healing magic into her body.

Finally, Wendi fell back into the soggy, blood-stained couch with a wet thud, whimpering and crying in pain, trying to curl into a ball. She would have succeeded in moving away from Mikel completely had it not been for the restraining hand he placed on her ribcage, pressing her tightly into place as he continued his prayers, his unstopping holy magic keeping her alive.

Her pain-filled cries began to subside as the cleric slowly made progress, gaining ground in the battle between healing and destruction. Her wounds began to open more slowly, becoming more ready to close even as they opened. After only a few more moments, fresh wounds ceased appearing altogether and he finally settled back, satisfied that Wendi would live. No more energy swirled, all of the trapped magic had either been reabsorbed into the necromancer or had been lost, escaping the area during the lifesaving ministrations.

Slowly, as Ahna and Mikel calmed from their combined exertion, the sounds of the conflict outside the inn reached their ears. During the time they had spent tending to Wendi, neither of them had paid any attention to the flow of battle, trusting in their friends and companions to keep them safe.

Her own task complete, Ahna drew a ragged breath, then stood and walked over to the window, hoping to see some signal that the fight was nearing its end. What she had hoped to see was nowhere near what was revealed as she looked upon the courtyard. Far from being almost over, the battle was still well underway. Witches and mages flung spell after spell at the defenders, who were in turn tied up with pirates and their wickedly lethal swords.

Explosions rocked the keep, rattling stone and shaking the buildings to their very foundations. Ahna fell back at the impact, sprayed with rubble from the stone wall as it buckled and sent a spray of minuscule stones into her. She crawled away from the wall as it crumbled, scraping both palms on the rough ground as she moved. The only barrier between the trio in the meeting room and the fight outside fell to the ground, seared and burned stones tumbling and rolling across the courtyard.

"There you are," Zavala turned to face them, her voice a singsong parody of friendliness. "I've been looking for you." She glided through the air towards her former companion, toes only inches above the ground.

Another explosion rocked the keep, disrupting Ahna's already tenuous balance. Bottles broke, fumes wafting over the group from an assortment of mixed concoctions, likely from the alchemical mixtures stored in the building next door to the one in which Ahna and Mikel were trapped. Beasts from the menagerie howled in the distance and Ahna absently wondered whether the howls were signals of pain from the creatures being attacked as well or whether they were howls of excitement as they had been freed to join the fray.

Wendi, curled into a ball finally, began roaring in pain once more in a voice that was no longer identifiable as human, the most terrible sound Ahna had ever heard. Her blood turned into ice water at the sound, pulse thundering in her ears with every beat of her panicked heart. A shout from outside, barely audible over Wendi's howling and her own pulse, directed her attention from the screaming necromancer and the approaching flier to the courtyard where skeletons began climbing up from the ground. At first one climbed from the soil, followed by a second, until dozens began appearing from every direction. The handful of pirates who hadn't lived to see the end of the battle rose as well, their deaths much less peaceful and restful than they had probably hoped for.

This must have been what it was like in Tomens, Ahna realized with a start. Hordes of undead, joined by the ranks of recently fallen. Bile rose in her throat as she watched the macabre sight with equal parts dread and fascination.

As they rose to unlife, the skeletons stayed where they appeared. None of them attacked, and after a brief moment, the shock of their arrival began to subside. The pirates and keep defenders alike began to cut away at the ancient undead, who did not defend themselves in any way as they were attacked.

The skeletons and other undead weren't the only ones being targeted. Spells cast from the Grand Coven and swords flashed from the pirates. Keep defenders, most of whom had already been injured, started losing ground as the tide of battle turned. Death was a fact of life for the pirates and the Grand Coven had far more experience with death magic than had any of the defenders so they were able to recover from their shock much more quickly.

Distracted by Wendi's screams, Sean glanced away from the pirate with whom he was entangled. As the group looked on in horror, the pirate seized the opportunity and slipped his blade through Sean's stomach. The red-haired man's eyes widened in surprise and he looked down to the end of the blade jutting from his body and then over to the grinning face of his killer. Slowly, the pirate withdrew his sword, bringing a gout of lifeblood in its wake.

The world fell silent.

Wendi's inhuman scream stopped as instantaneously as it had begun, leaving a deafening hush across the area. Even the sounds of clashing swords seemed muted, as though heard through a thick barrier. The feeling of magic, a deeper sensation than what had been caused by the spellcasting that had already been occurring, washed over the keep. Skin crawled and all who felt it recognized that a small portion of their souls had just been ripped away, willing or otherwise. Even those who practiced no magic recognized what was happening.

Wendi's eyes, blacker than the darkest night,

flew open. She stared into nothingness, focused on neither the people around her nor the area in which she continued to lay.

Every skeleton and undead in the courtyard who remained standing turned to face Sean as he slumped, lifeless to the ground. Their attention then turned to the pirate that killed him. Recognizing the danger in which he found himself, the pirate began to back away from the undead army, quickly finding himself surrounded with nowhere to retreat.

The skeletons reached out with bony, claw-like finders, grasping at him and digging into his flesh. One skeleton was joined by two, then by three. Inch by inch, the undead army began to peel the flesh away from the desperately screaming pirate. Slow, shambling steps brought more skeletons to bear, each of whom carried his own ounce of death to the hapless man.

Ahna felt all of her protective sigils flare simultaneously, a sensation she had never felt before. While she had felt multiple of them ignite, there had never been a time when she had required the use of all of them simultaneously. She couldn't imagine what kind of danger had just caused such an occurrence, confused as she was by the absolute and unyielding silence that surrounded the area. Along with the end of Wendi's screaming, the resounding clamor of sword against sword, the thunderous boom of powerful spells being thrust into the crowd had all ceased. Even the screaming from the pirate as he was torn limb from limb by the skeletons caused no sound.

As she watched in horror, blood began leaking from every magic user in the courtyard. The bloodletting was only the beginning, as their flesh began to slip from their bodies as well, dropping to the ground in shapeless chunks. Confused as to why she wasn't suffering the same mysterious effects, she noticed that the talisman she wore, the protective medallion been given to her by Faegan, the cleric in Sapphire, was glowing an intense blue. Looking around at her own group, she noted Magi Andress, wearing a similar charm. Phemie, bleeding from her eyes and ears, was hurriedly placing a charm of her own around her neck. She got it placed just in time, as one of the members of the Grand Coven began to melt away.

Terrified at this latest turn of events, the remaining pirates fled. Only seconds later, nothing more than an army of motionless skeletons and scattered puddles remained to show what had just transpired in the courtyard.

20

The next few days were a strange mixture between hurried repairs to the keep and its defenders and relaxed celebration of their successes. Crucian and Jaegar spent the majority of their time clearing away debris and restoring order to Dragon Keep, assisted heavily by Oree and Hannibal and under Phemie's watchful eye. The body parts Crucian had lost in the battle, the majority of one arm and half of an ear, were growing back quite nicely, although Ahna still didn't understand how. She had initially asked Mikel if he had cast a regenerative spell on the man but Mikel had assured him that was not the case.

Mikel, for his part, had spent the majority of his time tending to the wounded. Vox and Oree, both damaged in the battle, had been the first released to assist with the maintenance and repairs, followed soon by Hannibal, Keagan and Dominique. Although it had initially appeared to any who was watching that Sean had been killed in the attack, his wounds were no longer life threatening, although Mikel hadn't yet released him from his bed.

"He's going to pull through just fine," Mikel reassured Wendi for the hundredth time. "Yes, it looks bad and he's going to end up with a nasty scar but we got to him quickly enough that I was able to repair most of the internal damage before it got too far."

Once Wendi had calmed from the initial shock of seeing Sean fall, she had sent all of the skeletons back to their graves so there were no longer masses of undead hanging about to terrify any who hadn't already been scared off by the battle.

She and Ahna had barely exchanged words after their ordeal but Ahna didn't mind. There was nothing left to be said. What happened now, what Wendi chose to make of her life with her powers restored, was up to her. Even the missing memories that Wendi had so longed for had been restored. She just hoped that the necromancer decided to maintain her new lifestyle as mistress of Dragon Keep and purveyor of magical goods instead of returning to her previous life as a death mage under service to the Grand Coven. Regardless of what choices Wendi faced in her life from that point, the decisions were hers and hers alone.

Ahna had a similar decision to make. With the current threat no longer hounding her, she needed to decide what to do with her own life. She could, of course, return home to truly become the Countess de Melville. She could return to the Academy to resume her training. She was certain that, all things considered, Magi Andress and the rest of the Three Rivers Academy magi would be willing to overlook her absence and accept her as a student once more. She also had a third option, one she hadn't quite decided whether she wanted to explore further or not. She could continue her adventure, traveling with her new companions and learning more about the world beyond the manor's doors and the Academy's portcullis.

Although many of the Coven members had been killed in the assault, Ahna held no false hopes that the entire group had been destroyed in the battle. There had been less than two dozen members at the keep during the debacle, nowhere near the mass they could summon should they truly desire a war. Given how widespread the Coven's influence was, she strongly doubted that the battle had even made a dent in the Grand Coven's true strength.

"We need to talk." Jasika pulled Ahna's attention away from the bustle of activity. The assassin, obviously not one to let a battle happen in her vicinity without her becoming involved in it, had somehow managed joined the fray despite her own injuries. It had later been revealed that Jasika had been largely responsible for the quantity of undead pirates that had risen with Wendi's return to power. Even without the aide of her trademark swords and with wounds that should have killed her, the woman had still amassed an impressive body count. Ahna was beginning to understand why she was so feared throughout the three empires.

"What about?"

"Privately." Without waiting to see if Ahna would follow, Jasika stepped quietly toward the inn. The exterior wall, which had been damaged during the fight and had almost crushed Ahna as it fell, had been replaced, although the mortar holding the stones in place was not quite dried and set.

Equally nervous and curious, Ahna followed Jasika to the room that she and Keagan shared. Once inside, the assassin closed the door and secured it. "Do not fear," she reassured her. "I've no intention of killing you today."

She reached under the bed and pulled out a well-worn satchel. From the satchel, she withdrew a rough pine box, which she handed to Ahna.

Only the faintest trace of the etchings that had once covered the lid were still visible on the surface but Ahna immediately recognized the official seal of the emperor of the Dracott Empire. She looked up at Jasika in confusion.

Silently, Jasika reached under her tunic and withdrew a tiny key on a thin leather cord. She pulled it over her head and handed it to Ahna.

Ahna accepted the key and inserted it into the lock. With a soft click, the latch released. She lifted the lid and stared at its contents.

The box was lined with cream-colored silk, padded and shaped to securely cradle the item for which it had obviously been designed. A drinking horn, crafted from the horn of a unicorn and a pewter base inlaid with garnets were the box's only contents.

Ahna couldn't withhold a gasp of surprise as realization of what she held in her hands dawned on her. Although she had heard stories of the Horn of Ascension her entire life, as had almost everyone who had grown up in the Dracott Empire, she had never expected to see it in person, let alone to hold it in her hands. With no need for further confirmation, she knew that it was the genuine artifact. It practically vibrated with history. "You really do have it," she breathed. "This is amazing. It's even more beautiful than I ever imagined it to be." She traced a finger down one of the grooves where the horn spiraled toward the tip, amazed at how smooth the surface was.

"I also have this," Jasika added as she offered her a scroll, parchment sealed with red wax. "It's a writ of authenticity. That should negate any arguments about the validity of that object."

"How..." Ahna stumbled to find the correct words, too many questions were vying for attention in her head. "How did you keep them hidden for so long?"

"That's not something you need to worry about now."

"What are you going to do with them?" The contents of the box, as far as Ahna was aware, had never left the Dracott Empire, had never left the castle in Tomens. It was the most heavily guarded artifact in the entire empire, with hand-selected guards tasked with only its security at all hours of the day and night. Despite all the safeguards, it had somehow managed to arrive in the Inland Empire, in the possession of the most notorious outlaw of the Barberry Empire, precisely as Jasika had once said. Implications of that fact alone were almost unimaginable. By possessing the Horn of Ascension, Jasika was automatically the rightful ruler of the entire Dracott Empire. Although she hadn't yet traveled to Tomens to secure her position, Ahna knew that it was inevitable. "How can my house be of service to you?"

Jasika laughed for the first time since Ahna had met her, a surprisingly gentle and youthful sound. "You're acting as though I own that. I don't want it. I never wanted it. I had it for years without even knowing what it was." Suddenly, the notorious assassin, feared across three empires, appeared to be exactly what she was: a young girl not much older than Ahna herself.

Again, Ahna wondered what had transpired in Jasika's life to turn her into the killer she had become. "I don't understand," Ahna said. "If you don't want it, then what do you intend to do with it?"

"Nothing," the assassin answered simply. "It's not mine. In fact, it's not even in my possession anymore." She reached out and gently closed the lid, once more hiding the valuable treasure stored within. "I would suggest you not flash that thing to everyone on your way back home, though. People will kill to get their hands on an artifact like that. Believe me, I know."

Comprehension dawning, Ahna raised her eyes to Jasika's. "You can't be serious."

"I am absolutely serious. You've done all that you can do here. I think its high time you go home. I'm sure the Grand Coven will take a little while to recover from their recent loss and they have to accept that you aren't interested in joining them.

"As far as the pirates, well, I have plans for them yet. I still have a few things to resolve with their king." She spat out the last words with such venom that the now-familiar chill ran down Ahna's spine. She still didn't truly understand the relationship between the Pirate King and the Dark Star but, whatever it had once been, it was no longer good.

Ahna resecured the lock and tucked the precious key around her own neck. "I don't even know what to say," she admitted.

"Don't say anything. And, whatever you decide to do from here on, don't let anyone know from whom you got that. I've got a good life here on my own and I'd like to keep it that way." She turned back to the door, stopping with her hand on the latch. "Also, should you ever find yourself in danger, remember where I am. I'm not cheap, but I am worth every fouta."

The next morning, with Phemie's encouragement and despite the damage remaining at Dragon Keep yet to be repaired, Ahna, Vox, and Mikel headed for the transport gate, the aged and worn box carefully stored in Ahna's bag. She had restored her hair to its original golden tresses and wore her combs proudly. The clothes she had purchased in Hub, clothing to which she had grown accustomed on her travels, were stored in the bag as well. Instead of the rough cloth, she wore the silks she had worn on the day she left home to begin her training at the academy. They were halfway across the courtyard before Ahna recognized a familiar voice calling out after her.

"Wait up," Dominique jogged to catch up with them, satchel over her shoulder and rapier at her hip. "I leave you guys alone for five minutes to go grab my bag and you try to leave without me?" She smiled at Ahna in mock anger.

"I didn't realize you were serious about coming with us," Ahna admitted. The pair had grown closer than Ahna could have imagined in the short time they had known each other. She had to admit that she had been saddened by the idea of losing another dear friend and was pleased that Dominique had decided to join them after all.

"Of course I'm coming with you!" She took Ahna's arm in her own. "After everything you told me about your empire, I can't wait to see all of it."

With a smile, the foursome stepped through the gate, arriving immediately in Tradewinds. From there, they joined the long line to await their turn at the portal.

Two hours later, they arrived in Tomens, capital city of the Dracott Empire.

It was time for Ahna to start her rule.

The adventure continues in

Waters of Life

Available July, 2025

Keep reading for an exclusive sneak peek!

"This one is nice, I suppose."

"Yes, that is a good choice indeed. Made of the finest Gaon Ebony wood."

She ran her hand over the smooth, warm surface. For wood, carved from the trunk of a tree, it was surprisingly soft and smooth, as though it had been coated in the finest silk. The color was deep, fathomless black that seemed to absorb all of the available light, releasing none in reflection. Looking closely, she could see the grain but only faintly. "I'm not sure I like the idea of it being black. Can we look at something a little brighter, perhaps?"

"Of course. How about this one? Lacewood is a nice color, both pale and bright and it has such a lovely feminine pattern." He brought out a different sample, this one much paler with an almost orange hue. Lighter-colored splotches covered the surface in a pleasing, rhythmic pattern, no doubt leading to its name. To her, it looked more like ripples on the water during a blustery day than it did lace of any variety, but she hadn't been asked her opinion when naming the wood.

Keyt's mind was swimming through all of the options she had been given. Who knew there were so many different types of wood? Each of them was lovely in its own right, in almost every color found in nature and then others she hadn't been previously aware of. Some were polished to a high gloss and others were matte, softer and less shiny. They were all nice, any oof them she had been shown would work just fine, but none of them seemed to be what she wanted.

What she really wanted, if she was honest with herself, was to not be there, not be making the decision.

She closed her eyes, as though trying to block the scene before her, visually rejecting the decision she knew must be made. "The lacewood looks great, let's go with that."

"Wonderful, just wonderful. And for the interior?" Yet another of his endless boxes of samples joined the wooden pieces on the table.

Keyt was in no mood for more samples, more decisions she didn't want to make. "White satin," she said. "It's traditional and simple." The scent in the shop, intended to be warm, inviting, and soothing was instead cloying, clouding her already-addled senses and increasing the heaviness that had already spread throughout her body. She couldn't wait to get back outside in the fresh air where she could breathe freely but she couldn't leave until this task was done.

If she left now, she wasn't sure she would come back.

"Are you certain? We have so many lovely fabrics lately, I'm positive you will find something more to your liking." Already rifling through his new box of samples, he began pulling out small squares of fabric for her to inspect.

She shook her head. "No. White satin."

"All right," the salesman relented and placed the samples back into the box. "We can have this ready for you in just a few days. Is it an..." he paused, "urgent need?"

"A few days should be fine. She's not going anywhere."

As he tallied up the total due for her purchases, Keyt glanced around the showroom, her eyes moving from display to display, wondering which of the pieces in the showroom would end up hers when the time came.

Or, more likely, which of them she would end up purchasing for Malec when his time came as well.

"Brass finishings, I presume?" Unnoticed, the

salesman had pulled out another box of samples, his hand hovering just over the top of it as though he wasn't sure she wanted to see anything further.

"Of course," she replied automatically. Brass finishings or bronze, she didn't care. Even the wood she had selected didn't matter, nor did the satin upon which she had been so insistent. When all was said and done, none of the decisions she had made that day would have any impact on anything. Nobody would appreciate the time she had already spent agonizing over this decision, the choices she had made, wondering whether they were correct. Nobody would appreciate the constant need to swallow her stomach back into place at the smell of the flowers, vases stuffed with blooms and greenery that were everywhere.

When the shopkeeper explained the final total for her selection, she could have choked at the number. Perhaps she should have gone with a cheaper wood after all. She paused for a moment, wondering whether or not it was too late to change her mind on her choices. In the end, however, it didn't matter. She had made her decision and she would stand by it. After all, she could afford to pay his exorbitant price.

She counted out the tyros, carefully arranging them into orderly stacks of ten for him to confirm. Once all of the stacks had been placed on the counter, she added a trio of silver thalers to complete the transaction.

"You will deliver this, I assume?" She looked up to meet his eyes for the first time since her arrival at the shop. She certainly hoped that would be part of the purchase price, as she wasn't sure how she would handle it otherwise.

"Of course. Do not worry; we will take care of everything from here." As it had been throughout the whole conversation, his voice was low and modulating, meant to be soothing, but it did little to help Keyt's mood.

Satisfied, if not pleased, she tucked the purse back into her pocket, quickly walked across the showroom floor and stepped out the door onto the busy street beyond. She took a deep breath of the clean air, thankful that it no longer smelled of pungent flowers. Pedestrians walked past her, some in a hurry but most enjoying a lazy morning, in no rush to get from place to place. A handful of carts rattled down the street, pulled by horses who were equally unhurried. Across the street, children played tag, chasing each other around and laughing. The clouds that had covered the sky, delivering the early morning rains, had drifted further away, now small and peaceful in the distance.

As with most people, Keyt was dressed in warm furs to guard against the impending winter weather. Her thick boots, with heavy soles designed for slogging through the mud, were an exception to the norm in town but not unusual enough to warrant suspicious glances. Her long hair, the same shade of dark brown as almost everyone around her, hung down her back in a thick braid. A few tendrils came loose in the light wind and she tucked them behind her ears to keep them out of her face.

Keyt turned to walk down the street, her steps slow and steady as she went. Her mind was still murky, her thoughts filled with the activities of the past few days and wondering what she should do next. This had been her last stop, the task she had dreaded the most, and now her business was complete. There was nothing left for her to do, no further arrangements to be made, until the ceremony. She felt drained, as though she had spent the entirety of her life force over the last few days.

As prepared as she had believed herself to be, making all of the arrangements had been far more exhausting than she had expected.

The air held a thin tang, the annual promise of snow was still far off in the distance but headed closer every day. Soon, the streets and buildings would be covered in a heavy white winter blanket. The foxes and other summer creatures in the nearby forest would disappear, replaced by winter wolves and snow rabbits, animals more suited to the cold. She would have to go out into the woods soon as well, the traps needed to be checked and replaced before the snow arrived.

The sight of smoke, lazily drifting toward the clouds, welcomed her home. The house her family lived in, as with most houses in the area, was long and low, a single room that stretched from one end of the building to the next. From inside, she barely had to stretch in order to reach the roof overhead, which made simple work of the regular patching that it required. Fireplaces were set into either end of the house, both of which had been lit so to make the interior cozily warm and welcoming. Much as she wanted to go inside, the reindeer needed to be tended, so she walked around the house and to the open area beyond, heavy boots crunching through the light coating of frost that had settled over the valley following the morning shower.

"Hey, big fella." She reached out a hand toward the first big buck she encountered. This particular buck had been with her family for years and had sired many of the foals bouncing through the meadow. She walked through the herd, careful to not scare any of them and start a stampede. Although it had been years since she had made that mistake, the lesson had been well-learned and she hadn't needed a repeat lesson.

A couple of the foals were doing better than she had expected, each of them standing strong and tall already. These had been born late in the season and she had been worried on whether they would be strong enough to survive the winter, so seeing them up and agile already was heartening. One was still unsteady on its feet and she moved closer to examine it, concerned for both its health and its safety. "If you don't get a bit stronger soon," she explained, "the wolves will be able to catch you."

Of course, she knew the reindeer couldn't understand her. She wasn't capable of communicating directly with them, but she still felt as though they could understand what she meant. Something about their big brown eyes and the way they watched her as she went about her business held a sense of knowing, as though they comprehended far more than most realized. Whether it was true or not, she still spoke to them, letting them know what she was doing whenever she approached their pen or had to go inside for any reason. It was also because of that reason that she was particularly careful with her words whenever she brought one of the creatures to the slaughterhouse. The less the herd knew of what was happening, the better off they all were.

Once she finished examining the reindeer foals, satisfied that they were healthy and would continue to grow in both size and energy, she turned to head into the house. There were no windows to allow light in from outside, as all of the doors were covered with heavy skins in anticipation of the colder weather that had finally arrived. Malec waited inside, sitting in his favorite chair next to one of the fires and shuffling the embers with a poker. A black kettle was suspended just over the embers, high enough to not be touched by the flames when another log was added but low enough for the embers to keep its contents warm.

Malec was older than Keyt by one year, but he had a weak constitution and didn't leave home very often. While she tended to any business that brought her to town, he remained behind to care for the livestock, maintain the household and prepare the meals. Since he was inside, he wore only the lighter underlayers of clothing but he had a thick woolen blanket on his lap to keep the chill from his bones. Unlike the wide frame of most men of the northern lands, Malec was thin and appeared every bit as frail as he truly was.

"How did it go?" he asked when he saw her.

"About as well as it could have, I suppose."

He nodded quietly and watched as she picked up a bowl from the counter and ladled some soup from the kettle. "Any problems?"

"No," she shook her head. "Everything's arranged, so now all we need to do is wait for the ceremony." Her bowl filled, she carried it back to the counter to fetch a spoon.

"When is it scheduled for?"

"Four days from now. Everything will be delivered to the site and laborers will start on setting up the temporary framework tomorrow." She settled at the low table and sniffed, inhaling the rich scent. "This smells delicious."

He joined her at the table, matching bowl in hand, and they ate in silence. Occasionally the meal was interrupted by snippets of conversation, but those were few and far between. Long gone were the days of raucous conversation and arguments over the last heel of bread, the siblings were no longer children and no longer needed to act as such.

"I don't think I want to go," Malec said finally.

"You have to go," Keyt responded without hesitation. "It's mother. You can't just ignore this."

"I know." Frustration dripped from his voice. "It's not that I want to ignore this, I just don't know if I can handle it."

"You can." She reached a reassuring hand out to cover his. "You can and you will. I will be there to support you; I'll always be there for you. You know that."

"I just…" his voice broke. "I feel so lost right now."

"Me too. But I think that's normal." She passed him another piece of bread, along with a pat of freshly-churned butter. "And it's going to feel this way for a while but eventually things will return to normal."

Rather than responding, he picked up his bowl and hers, along with both spoons, and carried them over to the wash-bucket. "The worst part," he said once the dishes were clean, "is that, for us, this is normal. Completely, perfectly normal."

She couldn't argue with him. His words were true. Nothing either of them could do would change what had happened, nor could they change what was to come.

After life growing up in the beautifully rainy Pacific Northwest, Shanon L. Mayer tends to keep indoors, writing story after story, building vivid worlds on paper while her thoughts hold everything but images. She tends to look at everything in her world for inspiration – especially her collections of skulls, dragon statues, swords and knives, and pretty much anything that fits her eclectic, geeky-gothic lifestyle.

When her busy life feels like too much, she can be found relaxing with a hot mug of tea and a documentary on anything from theoretical physics to deep ocean wildlife to the most famous heists the world has ever seen.